ALSO BY ADAM SELZER

How to Get Suspended
and Influence People

PIRATES of the RETAIL WASTELAND

BY ADAM SELZER

delacorte press

Published by Delacorte Press
an imprint of Random House Children's Books
a division of Random House, Inc.
New York

Visit us on the Web! www.randomhouse.com/teens

Educators and librarians, for a variety of teaching tools,
visit us at www.randomhouse.com/teachers

Library of Congress Cataloging-in-Publication Data

Selzer, Adam.
Pirates of the retail wasteland / by Adam Selzer.
p. cm.
Summary: When eighth-grader Leon decides what to do for his project in the
gifted program, it involves coffee houses, pirates, and filmmaking.
ISBN 978-0-385-73482-0 (trade) — ISBN 978-0-385-90480-3 (lib. ed.)
[1. Gifted children—Fiction. 2. Motion pictures—Production and direction—
Fiction. 3. Middle schools—Fiction. 4. Schools—Fiction.] I. Title.
PZ7.S4652Pi 2008
[Fic]—dc22
2007027602

The text of this book is set in 12-point Goudy.

Printed in the United States of America

10 9 8 7 6 5 4 3 2 1

First Edition

For Howard.
No hard feelings, man,
but enough already!

Many thanks to Nadia, my fantastic agent, to Stephanie, my wonderful editor, and to Colleen, the copy editor by whom nothing gets. Also, thanks to Nancy Angelopoulos and everyone at the real Sip Coffee on Grand Avenue in Chicago, to Jen Hathy and everyone at the Mercury Cafe (near Ashland and Chicago), and to Carol White (for all that tea at the Java Monkey in Atlanta). And thanks to all the good people I worked with in my years as a McHobo (during that long period when minimum wage remained stuck at $5.15). Also, of course, heartfelt thanks to my family, who drove me to and from work on the many, many days when my car wasn't running.

It's getting harder and harder to get a bad cup of coffee . . . and damn it, I'm mad!
—Tom Waits

There are rare times when school isn't such a bad place to be, and chief among these are the times when you're sitting on a couch with a girl's butt pressed into each of your arms.

Granted, this isn't the sort of thing that happens every day, but it was known to happen to me on Fridays during the gifted-pool meetings. At the first meeting of the second semester of my eighth-grade year, all twelve of us were piled onto the old green couch in the room above the gym, as was our usual fashion, while Mr. Streich, our fearless leader, took attendance.

I was trying to pay attention to what was going on. Or, anyway, I was trying to look like I was—but I had Anna Brandenburg's butt pressing into the lower part of my right arm and Jenny Kurosawa's butt near my left shoulder, which was somewhat distracting. It's hard to imagine a situation more preferable to math class, where I spent sixth period the other four days of the week.

Mr. Streich was at the front of the room, running his fingers across his mustache—he did that quite a lot, as though he was trying to make sure it was still there or something—and pointing his pen at odd spots on the couch, trying to figure out if we were all present. It was no small task, considering that a couple of people were buried so deep that all he could see of them was their shoes. But he took it in stride.

"Well then," he said, when he had decided we were all there, "are you guys ready to hear what the first gifted-pool project of the semester is going to be?"

The noise that came out of the couch probably just sounded like a low rumble, but most of us were saying "Sure," "Yeah," or something like that.

"Your first project . . . ," Mr. Streich said, pausing to let the suspense build, as though we were all on the edge of our seats, "will be to create . . . a monument!"

For a second, no one said a word. This wasn't the kind of announcement that would get people cheering or anything, but from the look on his face, Mr. Streich had clearly expected *some* kind of reaction. I figured I ought to say something before he started to feel bad. We liked Mr. Streich just about enough to try not to hurt his feelings.

"A monument?" I asked. "What kind of monument are we talking about here?"

"Well," he said, "it can be anything. You'll each pick someone or something that you think deserves a monument, and build the monument yourself. Then you'll present it at an assembly, as usual."

This didn't sound much different than the project from

the previous semester where we had to dress up like some notable person from history and give a speech about their life—most of the projects were something along this line. The school was careful not to give us projects that might lead us to blow anything up or incite any riots; even the "dressing up as a notable person from history" assignment had led to a veritable spree of cross-dressing. Dustin Eddlebeck had only been stopped from dressing as Sally Rand, a notable stripper who used to dance wearing nothing but a large fan, at the last second by some chumps from the school board.

I'm not exactly sure how they came to decide that those of us in the pool were "gifted." You normally think of the gifted kids as the ones who tuck their shirts into their underwear and spend their free time talking to their plants about algebra. At my school, it was mostly a bunch of miscreants—commies, perverts, and pyros who happened to score well on standardized tests.

"How about a gravestone?" asked James Cole, who spoke fluent French and was the first kid in school to smoke pot. "Would that be considered a monument?"

"Well," said Mr. Streich, "maybe you could make a gravestone for someone who didn't have one, and try to have it actually put up where they're buried! I've heard of people doing that for old blues singers who were just dumped under a plywood marker someplace."

"Actually," said James, "I was thinking about one for Coach Hunter."

Coach Hunter was the gym teacher, and James Cole's natural enemy. If anyone ever makes one of those public television nature documentaries about potheads, it'll probably have a scene of them pricking up their ears and getting scared when they hear a whistle blowing in the distance.

"Coach Hunter isn't dead," Mr. Streich pointed out, as if we didn't already know that.

"I know," said James. "I was thinking we would have to kill him as part of the project."

We all laughed, and Mr. Streich tried to calm us down, though I could see that he was trying not to smile. "I don't think he'd be very keen on that, James."

"Well," I said, "you're supposed to be challenging us to use our gifted intellects, right? Why not challenge us to spend the semester convincing Coach Hunter that life isn't worth living anymore? That way, we wouldn't have to kill him ourselves."

"Heck," said James. "It probably won't even take that long. I start thinking life isn't worth living after about five minutes in his class."

"We could learn a lot about psychology," said Edie Scaduto, the school communist.

"You guys, be serious for a minute," said Mr. Streich. "You *know* I can't let you kill anybody, and I certainly can't let you try to convince anybody to kill themselves, because if I could, I would have assigned you to take out my mother-in-law by now." He paused for us to laugh, which we did, a little. It might have been funnier if he were married in the first place. "If you want to make a monument like the Tomb of the Unknown Gym Coach, that might be okay. Just be careful."

Mr. Streich may have been the last man alive to use the

word "keen," but he wasn't such a bad guy, really. He was about a million times better than Mrs. Smollet, his predecessor, who spent most of the meetings going off about how we all lacked family values and moral fiber, until I'd finally pissed her off so badly the previous semester that she'd quit the job. At the time, Mr. Streich had been teaching the "advanced studies" morning activity, where we'd been assigned to make a health or safety film to show to the younger kids. My entry, an avant-garde sex-ed film called *La Dolce Pubert*, had frightened Mrs. Smollet so badly that she'd had me suspended for it. Shortly thereafter, she'd resigned, and Mr. Streich took her place.

Mr. Streich wasn't as easy a target for us, partly because he didn't find us quite as shocking or terrifying as Mrs. Smollet did. Every time she saw us piled up on the couch in one big heap, she was ready to march us to the nurse's office to have us checked for STDs.

"Leon," he said, picking my face out of the lump on the couch, "maybe you could make a monument to Thomas Edison. I'm sure your dad would love that." He grinned.

"Ho, ho, ho," I said.

Mr. Streich was a science teacher by trade, and was a friend of my father, who was an accountant who wished he were an inventor. Hating Thomas Edison's guts is sort of Dad's hobby. He even gave me the middle name Noside ("Edison" spelled backwards) as some sort of insult to his memory. I can only assume that sane people don't do this sort of thing to their kids.

"I know," said Anna, who was a little next to me and a little on top of me in the pile, with her butt now against my upper arm, near my shoulder. "You could do a monument to the elephant Edison killed!"

"Great idea!" said Mr. Streich. And he grabbed a marker and wrote "dead elephant" on the board.

Edison once tried to prove that his competitor's brand of electricity was dangerous by using it to electrocute an elephant. Seriously. I hate to admit my dad is right about anything, but it's true that Edison had some serious issues.

"Anyone else have some good ideas for things that need a monument?" asked Mr. Streich. "Just shout them out."

"Karl Marx," said Edie. Mr. Streich shrugged and wrote it on the board. Mrs. Smollet probably would have made a real stink about that one, but Mr. Streich was a lot better at picking his battles.

"Nikola Tesla," said Brian Carlson. Brian was Edie's boyfriend, and while he wasn't a science genius or anything, he was pretty good at turning ordinary objects like pens and address labels into deadly weapons. He wasn't really the violent type; a determined third grader could probably kick his ass. But many of the local office supply stores had his picture up behind the counter above the words "Do not sell to this boy," and some people said that the reason the school had never made a big deal about having a zero-tolerance weapons policy was that they knew that as long as Brian was allowed to have a pencil, there would always be weapons.

After a few minutes, we'd suggested monuments for Chef Boyardee, Satan, Captain Hook, the Trix rabbit, and Jim Morrison, the lead singer of the Doors. No one knew exactly how Jenny Kurosawa, whose parents didn't let her read or listen to anything that wouldn't look good on a college application, had become an obsessive Doors fan, but ever since Thanksgiving break, she'd worn a Doors T-shirt every day, and she'd taken to carrying around an empty Mountain Dew bottle on which she'd written "Jim Morrison's Soul" with a permanent marker where the label used to be.

One of Mrs. Smollet's catchphrases had been "This is the gifted pool, not the weirdo club." Clearly, she'd been fighting a losing battle.

When the bell rang, we all slowly worked our way off of the couch. Anna grabbed me by the arm.

"Basketball game tonight?" she asked.

"Of course," I said. "Brian and Edie coming?"

"I assume so."

Brian, overhearing, looked over and gave me the thumbs-up with one hand while he tried to get his hair out of his face with the other.

Going to the basketball game—the first few minutes of it, anyway—was one of our regular winter habits. We'd meet up at the high school, where we'd stay until we were sure my parents had driven away, then leave and spend an hour or two roaming around the town until it was about time for the game to be over, at which point we'd head back. Sometimes we went to the Laundromat to play their old Pac-Man machine, sometimes we went to a coffee shop, and sometimes we just hung around the park, making prank calls from the pay phone. It was without question the highlight of my week.

Anna and I were going out. Sort of. In a way. Neither of us had ever officially declared that we were a couple or anything like that, and when someone asked me if we were, I sort of danced around the issue. But we were more than just friends. Or, anyway, we made out from time to time. We'd filmed a kissing scene for *La Dolce Pubert*, and the next avant-garde film we made, *The Rooster in the Skating Rink: A Musical (Based on a True Story)*, had a whole bunch of kissing scenes. Every now and then, we even kissed when we *weren't* on camera. Not as often as I would have liked, but it was kind of a tricky situation—I mean, what if I asked her out officially and she got freaked out? It could make things weird between us forever. I worried about this sort of thing a whole lot more than I worried about my grades.

We all headed out the front door of the school. Edie, Brian, and practically everybody else headed for the buses. Anna and I both walked home. We normally walked together as far as the end of the parking lot, then went our separate ways.

"So I'll meet you tonight?" I asked, trying to look her in the eye, though that was sort of tough, as her head and face were covered up by her furry hood. It was like looking at someone through a thick, fuzzy veil.

"Yeah," she said. "But I've got something for you first."

"Oh yeah?" I asked.

"Yeah." She grinned evilly, pulled back her hood, and grabbed me by the back of my head. She pulled me closer to her, then attached her lips to my neck. For a second I was so startled that I didn't know how to respond, and even when I came to my senses, I wasn't sure what to do. I couldn't kiss her back, since she had my face pointed away from her and was sucking so hard that I couldn't really move. It actually hurt a bit, but I couldn't bring myself to squirm away, even when I heard a passing car honk at us.

Then, all of a sudden, she let me go. I moved in to kiss her back, but she backed up and grinned again.

"Have a good evening," she said sweetly. And she ran off across the street, cutting through somebody's backyard to get to the neighborhood on the other side of the street.

I was about halfway home before I realized what must have happened—she'd given me a hickey. And now I'd have the distinct pleasure of hiding it from my parents. This was probably her idea of a great joke—and I must admit that I liked her sense of humor.

For the life of me, I wasn't sure why Anna would be with a guy like me. For my money, she was the coolest person in school. Even her parents, who she called by their first names, were cool—her dad was a professor of eighteenth-century European history at the college in the city, and her mom was an art authenticator who flew all around the world doing tests on paintings to find out if they were real works by famous artists or just old paintings by some nobody.

Neither of these seemed like jobs people in the suburbs ought to have. In my head, art authenticators lived in cool old town houses in Manhattan with chamber music playing all the time, but Anna and her parents just lived in a regular split-level house on Horton Street. When I was in her house, surrounded by weird paintings and shelves full of books about rich jerks from the eighteenth century, I found myself wanting to make something of my life, something extraordinary, far away from Cornersville Trace. My parents tended to decorate with pictures of babies sitting in flower-pots. Those made me want to live far away, too, but for very different reasons.

I went into my house through the side door without calling out "I'm home" or anything like that, then made for the stairs and crept up them with the kind of swiftness normally found only in ninjas. I thought I was being pretty sneaky, but a minute later I heard my mother calling me.

"Leon?" she called. "Come down here for a second, will you?"

"In a minute," I called back. I looked over at the mirror—yep. There it was, all right. A hickey. Super. Normally I'd be thrilled that Anna had done something like that, as it was a pretty clear sign that she really did like me, but she could have at least waited until a day when I was wearing a turtleneck or something. I couldn't help wondering if maybe she really didn't like me and had done it just to be mean.

"Leon, come on down," said my father's voice. "I have something to show you."

I wondered what my father was doing at home. Normally he didn't get back from the accounting office on Fridays until five or six, at least.

"In a minute," I shouted as I dug through my dresser for something with a better collar.

I assumed that they just wanted to show me some new cookbook they'd found. My parents are "food disaster hobbyists," which means they get their jollies by buying old cookbooks and cooking the absolute worst recipes they can find, then making fun of them. It wouldn't be so bad, except that they also make a point of dressing up and acting like the people in whatever cookbook they're using at the moment. It's their concept of a family bonding experience, and my concept of torture.

Finally, my mother opened my door.

"What are you doing, Leon?" she asked, raising an eyebrow.

"Geez, Mom!" I shouted, looking up from the drawer. "Would it kill you to knock?"

"Sorry," she said. "But come downstairs. We have to show you something."

I walked down the stairs, carefully standing on the side of my mother that left her facing the nonhickey side of my neck. Not that hickeys were forbidden or anything like that, but I knew my mother would go on and on about how "cute" it was. She had a real talent for thinking things were cute.

Downstairs, my father was sitting at the kitchen table, wearing a ski mask that made him look like a bank robber. Maybe he was home early because he'd started a new career as a suburban mugger. The accounting world would certainly drive *me* to a life of crime.

"Hi, Leon," he said. I could see him grinning even through the mask.

"Hi," I said. "What's with the mask? Did you stay home from work to hold up the Quickway?"

"How was school today?" he asked, ignoring the question and still grinning like an idiot.

"Same as always," I said. "Nothing out of the ordinary."

He chuckled. "Can't say the same for my day at work."

Well, no kidding, I thought. People who have normal days at work usually come home *without* ski masks on. "What happened?"

I'd always suspected that my dad might be a bit unstable—I mean, anyone who gives a kid a first name like Leon—not to mention a middle name like Noside—after 1964 can't possibly be playing with a full deck.

I wondered if maybe my father had finally tipped over the edge, gone to work in a ski mask, and busted the place up with a crowbar. Every possible reason I had in mind for his wearing the ski mask involved violent crime in one way or another. It seemed like my mother wouldn't be smiling so much if he had done a thing like that, but then again, it'd be just like her to see bloodstains on the wall of the office and think they were "cute." I could imagine her pointing at big blotches of blood and saying "Oh, honey! That one looks like a choo-choo train, and that one looks like a bunny!"

"Well," said Dad, "in the middle of working on some accounts, I got an idea for a new invention, and took a personal day to come home at noon and work up a prototype. I've been out in the garage half the day working on it. And I don't mind saying that it's freezing in there."

"Hence the ski mask?"

"Nope. The ski mask was just so I wouldn't spoil the surprise." My mother was covering her mouth with her hand, trying not to laugh.

"What surprise?"

"This!"

With that, he whipped off the ski mask, and I just about died.

My dad's brown hair, which had formerly covered his entire head, had been replaced by a single strip of green hair down the center of his scalp. A Mohawk. And a green one, at that. And not just sort of a green tint, like my grandmother sometimes ends up with, but bright, neon green, so bright that he could have used it to guide Santa's sleigh on a foggy Christmas Eve.

I stared at it for a second.

My parents both broke out laughing.

"You got a Mohawk," I said, finally.

"How 'bout your old man?" he asked. "I look like a regular wild and crazy guy."

All I could do was stare.

My father was not a wild and crazy guy. He was certainly crazy, of course, but I've seen wilder houseplants. I imagine that when he was a kid, the wildest thing he ever did was probably buying *Archie's Double Digest* instead of the regular-sized Archie comics on days when he felt especially saucy. Even now, with a Mohawk, he didn't look terribly wild. He looked like a guy who'd just been beaten up by a gang of toughs who gave him a makeover while he was unconscious. Or like some guy who had been in a band thirty years ago and was now making a fool of himself trying to crack the nostalgia market.

"Well?" my father asked. "What do you think?"

"It . . . it's certainly different."

"Oh, Leon!" said my mother. "The look on your face is just priceless!"

"Does this make you the first accountant ever to have a Mohawk?" I asked.

"Probably," he said. "You might say I'm a regular pioneer."

"And they'll let you go to work looking like that?" I asked.

"Well, they might be upset, but they know they'd be lost without me. When you make yourself invaluable, there's no limit to what you can do." I thought I recognized this from one of the motivational speech recordings he played in the car.

"So this is your invention?" I asked. "Being an accountant with a Mohawk?"

"Not exactly. The invention is a new kind of hair dye—it'll only dye hair, and just rolls off every other surface."

I looked at the skin around his Mohawk and saw that there were plenty of green stains all over his scalp.

"Doesn't look like you've quite worked out all the kinks yet," I said.

"Well"—he grinned—"obviously not. But it at least dyed the hair, so I'm on my way!"

I sat down and just stared for a second. My dad had a green Mohawk. This was quite a lot to consider. Like, did this mean they'd let *me* get a Mohawk? Or pierce any part of my face?

I was so busy staring that I didn't notice that my mother was walking around to the other side of the table.

"And what have we here?" she asked, looking at my neck. "I do believe our young man has a hickey!"

Crap. So much for my ninja skills. I put my coat back on, trying to cover it up, fixing her with the most vicious look I could manage.

"Shut up," I said. "Just shut the hell up."

Normally my mother didn't like me using words like "hell," but I guess she was in the mood to find that cute, too.

"Don't be bashful," Dad said. "No one said you weren't allowed to get hickeys."

"I think it's precious," said my mother, while I fought the urge to barf, even though I'm sure she would have found that cute, too. "Our little boy is growing up."

"Was it Anna?" Dad asked.

"No," I said quickly. "We were working with vacuum engines in science, and one got stuck on my neck."

"Sure it did," said my mother. "Sure it did."

"Listen," I said to change the subject. "I'm gonna need a ride to the basketball game later tonight."

"That's fine," said my mother. "I figured on making dinner early so you could eat with us. You'll never believe what I found at the thrift store earlier today!"

I silently braced myself for the worst. The local thrift store was like a bottomless treasure chest full of cookbooks featuring awful-looking food from pretty much every decade. People in the 1950s were apparently obsessed with using Jell-O in everything, and, try as I might, I've yet to determine what people in the 1970s were thinking.

Sure enough, she handed me a cheap, spiral-bound book called *True Americans Are Grilling Americans*. On the cover was a blurry picture of a dirty-looking fellow wearing an American-flag apron and holding up a skewer with a chunk of meat on the end. At least, I hoped it was meat. If I hadn't known it was a book about grilling, I would have thought it was a picture of a hillbilly who had just been fishing in a Porta Potti and was now proudly holding up the catch of the day.

"Yuck," I said.

"And look at the title!" My mother beamed. "It sounds like a cookbook for patriotic cannibals!"

"Ha!" Dad laughed. "Patriotic Americans only grill other Americans! Only dangerous terrorists are grilling Canadians these days."

"Isn't it nasty?" Mom asked, handing me the book.

I flipped through it and saw that it was full of things like rabbit burgers, beaver skewers, and things like that. Either it was a cookbook for people who hunted for food near their own houses or for people who cooked roadkill—it didn't really specify how you were supposed to get the meat. There were no pictures, and most of it looked like it was made from cheaply copied typewriter pages. Obviously, it had been self-published. By someone who thought "charcoal" was spelled "charcole."

"We're not actually going to eat this stuff, are we?" I asked. "I mean, they don't sell squirrel meat at the grocery store, do they?"

"We'll mostly just use beef instead," said my mother. "But take a look at the recipes themselves—they're hardly even recipes. You just grill the meat and add ketchup to most of them. Some of them have you mix the ground meat and ketchup together before you grill it."

I said that I had homework to do as a means of escaping to my room—though I had no intention of actually doing my homework until I was back in class on Monday, in the fi-

16

nal minutes before the bell rang. If I did it at home, I'd just forget to bring it, anyway. The real purpose of being in my room was so that they wouldn't try to get me involved in cooking the meal. When they do food disasters, one of the rules is that they have to put on outfits from the decade or region in which the cookbook was published.

Sure enough, when I finally came downstairs, they were in "Grilling Americans" outfits. My mother had her hair messed up and was wearing a flannel shirt and torn jeans. My father was wearing a plain white T-shirt, a backwards John Deere baseball cap, and an American-flag apron of his own. At least the cap covered up the Mohawk. I wondered if getting a ketchup stain on the apron would be considered desecrating the flag.

My father was getting the meat ready while my mother sat on the couch, shouting at the television. Every now and then she'd turn and shout something at my father, who she was calling "Lester" for some reason.

"Lester!" she shouted. "Come see what they're givin' away on *Wheel of Fortune!*"

"Can it, Wanda!" Dad shouted back, though my mother's name is Judith. "Why don't you just stifle there and bring me a damn beer?" He then bundled up and took the meat out to the grill on the back porch, shouting something about how it was never too cold for a True American to grill.

On most food disaster nights, they spent the meal itself talking like normal people, just making fun of the food, but they apparently liked being Lester and Wanda so much that they kept it up right through dinner.

"Wanda, your fries taste like garbage," Dad grumbled.

17

"How do you expect a man to eat this?" The fries were indeed garbage, but she could hardly be blamed. They were the frozen, skinny kind of fries, which probably couldn't be saved.

"Oh, come off it, Lester," my mom said. "You couldn't grill a hot dog if you had an automatic hot dog machine that was approved by the national hot dog council." She leaned in closer to me. "Don't mind Lester," she said. "He ain't been quite right ever since he had all them worms removed from his butt."

Needless to say, I avoid having friends over for dinner whenever possible.

I don't really know which prospect was more frightening—
that my dad might drive me to the basketball game still talking like "Lester," or that he'd have the baseball cap off and
the Mohawk in plain sight. I would have given anything to
just walk to the high school, but my mother would barely let
me walk as far as the mailbox when it was dark outside, and
certainly wasn't about to let me walk all the way to the high
school, since, in her imagination, the suburbs were crawling
with gangbangers, pedophiles, and other undesirables who
hid in the bushes by day, then crawled out and roamed the
streets as soon as the sun went down.

To my great relief, Dad did the sensible thing and put on
a knit cap to cover his head as we got into the car.

"Covering up the Mohawk?" I asked.

"Well, it's about ten degrees Fahrenheit out there," he
said. "And I'm not used to having so much skin on my head
exposed. I don't want to freeze to death."

"That's very wise," I said, putting on a knit cap of my own that was large enough to cover my ears. I knew I'd be spending most of the night outdoors.

We drove out of the house and turned down Eighty-second Street to get to Tanglewood Parkway.

"You know," I said, "if I were walking, I could just go straight down August Avenue and be right at the school. You know I wouldn't get lost or anything."

"We know." Dad sighed. He was a little more sensible than my mother when it came to imaginary criminals. "But there's snow and ice all over the ground. You might slip and fall in the dark, and we wouldn't even know you were hurt until you froze to death."

"When was the last time anybody froze to death in this town?" I asked. "It's suburbia, not a little house on the prairie. Surely one of the muggers or drug dealers would come along to help me."

"Forget it, Leon," he said. "Maybe next year, when you're in high school, you'll be able to walk, but for now, it's out of the question."

My dad may have been a bit more progressive than my mom—he didn't really care if I walked home from Fat Johnny's, the pizza place on Eighty-second Street, just a few residential blocks away, after dark or anything like that. My dad's biggest concern was that the minute I was not under adult supervision, I'd be approached by every drug dealer in the state and wouldn't have the willpower to say no. As though I could possibly afford drugs on my allowance.

"Be careful," he said as we pulled into the parking lot.

"You know I will, Dad," I said.

20

"I know you're a good kid, Leon," he said. "We just want you to be careful. I know all about how tough peer pressure can be."

"Dad," I said, "I don't know what it was like when you were a kid, but when someone offers you drugs, they're usually just offering to be polite."

"Well," he said, "you know what to do if the situation comes up."

"Sure," I said. "Save some for you. See ya!"

At the door of the high school gym, I paid two bucks to get in and found Brian and Edie already standing around by the concession stand.

"Hey, guys," I said. "You want any drugs?"

"I don't know," said Brian. "What kind of drugs can I afford for four bucks?"

"Oh, I can get you all kinds of stuff for four dollars," I said. "Didn't you guys meet all the dealers hanging out on Tanglewood Parkway when you walked over here?"

"Yeah," said Brian. "And they tried to get us to join their gangs, but we just said no and ran."

"Good job," I said. "Sometimes when you're in a gang, they'll ask you to smoke."

I suppose we were exaggerating a bit—the town wasn't *that* clean. James Cole may have been the first kid in school to smoke pot, but plenty of kids had done it since then. And I knew that plenty of kids at the high school were living on the chronic diet—a joint for breakfast, another for lunch, and then a sensible dinner, like animal crackers and cheese puffs. Whenever anyone mentioned potheads, Edie would go into a rant about how, to afford drugs, they had to be rich

21

kids and should therefore be considered scum. Commies hate rich kids. Edie herself was not exactly poor—her parents were lawyers. But she claimed to have renounced them and everything they stood for.

A minute later Anna turned up, and we all sat down at one of the metal picnic tables set up near the concession stand and watched everybody coming and going. A few people we recognized from classes gave us the "I acknowledge you exist" nod, but they were all actually interested in the basketball game, and headed straight in for the stands, which were farther inside than we normally got. Per our custom, as soon as "The Star-Spangled Banner" was over, we were out the door. My mother would have been furious to know that I was actually spending the basketball games walking around town, but what she didn't know couldn't hurt her.

As usual, we headed south, cutting through Da Gama Park. Sometimes we stopped at the pay phone near the gazebo—practically the last pay phone in all of Cornersville Trace—to make prank phone calls, since pay-phone calls are a lot harder to trace than normal calls, but it was cold enough to freeze a guy's nuts off, and I didn't consider my nuts to be a reasonable sacrifice for a prank call.

On the other end of Da Gama Park was the little triangle made up of Venture Street, Douglas Avenue, and Seventieth Street, which, when I was a kid, was the main downtown area. Now, though, we called it the old downtown. Most of the stores there were closed up; nobody really went there anymore, since all of the new strip malls had gone in on Cedar Avenue. It seemed like people hardly even went to the regular mall anymore.

As we walked down Douglas, the diagonal street, we passed Cornersville Grocery, the little grocery store that no one had ever gone to. It had been the first business to close down, and had been sitting empty for years now. An old-timey sign painted on the window said SINCE 1957, and under that some joker had scribbled in "until 2002" with a perma-nent marker. It might as well have been a gravestone for the old downtown—all around the triangle, and all down Venture Street, there were hollowed-out shells of stores that had closed and never reopened.

But Sip, the coffee shop on Venture Street, was still in business, and had become our usual base of operations out-side of the gifted-pool room and Fat Johnny's. Friday nights were the open mike nights, and though there were usually only two or three people with anything to read or play, Dustin Eddlebeck, poet laureate of the middle school men's room wall, was almost always one of them. We thought it was important that we be there to support him.

Inside, Sip had the look of a basement that someone had started trying to turn into a rec room in about 1982 but never quite finished. Its walls were the same shade of green as my grandmother's teakettle, there was artwork painted by customers on the walls, and most of the lighting came from the little stained-glass lamps that hung from the ceiling at odd angles. Some were low enough that you hit your head if you weren't careful. A sign on the wall invited mean people to "piss off," and now and then there would be a cat on one of the tables. I suppose you could say it was the last bohemian enclave in suburbia.

Some kind of classical music with accordions was coming out of the speakers mounted on some bookshelves. I thought it sounded like a tango, which meant that Trinity, our favorite waitress, was probably working that night. She went to the high school, and dreamed of running away to become a ballroom dancer—she was into tango, in particular, because it was so sexy that the Pope once declared it a mortal sin.

When things were slow around the shop, she was often seen tango dancing across the store with an invisible partner. Officially, though, she was a punk rocker. Her hair was dyed deep blue, and though she dressed in vintage ball gowns most nights, she had them covered in safety pins and punk rock buttons.

Dustin and James were already there at one of the larger tables, and we sat down to join them.

"Evening, escapees," said Dustin. Neither he nor James bothered to show up at the basketball game ahead of time—if they'd said they wanted to go to a sporting event, their parents would have known right away that they were up to something.

"*Bonsoir*, butt-sticks," said James. If it wasn't the French that qualified him as gifted, it was probably his genius at inventing his own slang terms. The guy was an artist.

"What's happening?" I asked.

"We were just talking about my class project," said James.

"The one about Coach Hunter?" Anna asked. They both smiled.

24

"That thing about getting him to kill himself over the course of the semester was a masterstroke, Leon," said Dustin.

"You guys *do* know I wasn't serious, right?" I asked. "I was just messing around."

"Of course we do, ass monkey," said James. "But we happen to think you were on to something. We probably can't get him to kill himself, but maybe we can depress him so much that he'll pull a Mrs. Smollet and resign."

"I'm in charge of the depressing poetry," Dustin said, twirling a pen like a baton. "I can make most of the depressing poets in the literature anthologies look like Groucho Marx."

Dustin had spent sixth grade writing naughty limericks on the bathroom wall, and in seventh grade he had graduated to writing naughty sonnets, which were much longer. He'd written a pair of sonnets that had served as the narration for *La Dolce Pubert*. Shortly thereafter, he'd gotten interested in Rudyard Kipling, whom he described as a "hard-core badass" who wrote things like

When you're wounded and left on
Afghanistan's plains,
And the women come out to cut
up what remains,
Jest roll to your rifle and blow out your brains
An' go to your Gawd like a soldier.

He was really into that for about a week, until someone described Kipling as "the kind of poetry your gym teacher might write." It was true; his poems tended to go on and on about how to "be a man, my son," and you could easily imagine him shooting you in the knees and telling you to walk it off. After that, Dustin quietly renounced "badass poetry" and discovered free verse and beatnik poetry, which was rambling and weird and tended to be about walking around the city, having sex, and drinking coffee with jazz musicians. I think the day the first beatnik poem appeared on the bathroom wall, all the teachers took a field trip to the nearest church to pray for their lives.

A minute after we sat down, Trinity came to the table.

"You hoodlums again," she said, sounding thrilled. "You want the usual?"

We all nodded. Small cups of coffee all around.

Trinity nodded and brought out our drinks, the pins on her dress rattling all the way. She acted like she hated us, but we sort of suspected she liked us better than she liked most of the customers. Edie practically worshipped her—she thought that covering ball gowns with pins made a profound statement of some sort, and for once, I think she might have been on to something. Shortly after meeting Trinity, she'd gotten into punk rock, which she considered appropriately communist friendly, and had dyed bright red highlights into her black hair.

Anna had practically been bottle-fed on coffee, and she and her father had made it sort of a mission to get me into it. When I'd started drinking it, I was filling up my cups with more cream and sugar than actual coffee, but I was trying to wean myself off the cream until I could drink it black, like Anna did. I was getting pretty close.

The coffee at Sip was not the "gourmet" kind, but Anna

and her parents were of the opinion that "bad" coffee was actually a lot better. There was a certain taste that coffee could only acquire by sitting in the urn for a really long time. And anyway, those jazz guys in the fifties probably weren't drinking coffee made from only the highest-quality Colombian beans. They were drinking sludge.

A few minutes later, Dustin asked Trinity to turn down the music so he could read his latest poem, which he'd been scribbling on a napkin. She nodded, and took the stage herself.

"Ladies and gentlemen," she said, as though she were announcing that they would be closing down due to a gas leak, "it is with deepest regret that I subject you all to the poetic stylings of Mr. Dustin Eddlebeck." Dustin stood up to bow, then walked to the mike.

"I'd like to read a new piece," he said, "entitled 'The Final Push-up.' "

He cleared his throat and began to read.

"O Coach, where is thy sting?
At the bottom of the empty bottle
of Gatorade, the last few drops are
turning into crust,
like the last drops of blood
in your cold heart,
pumping slowly, like
a seven-hundred-pound sixth grader
trying to do that third and
final push-up,
wobbling a bit

and then crumpling on the mat
like a crushed paper cup,
discarded, scattered to the four winds,
et où sont les neiges, et où sont les neiges?
If it's better to burn out than fade away
like an athlete dying young on the finish line,
his heart bursting like a sudden solo
in a Miles Davis record,
then it's better to put your head in the oven
just like Sylvia Plath, who never
did a sit-up to my knowledge,
than to dry up like the last few drops
of aforementioned blood,
sitting in your wheelchair,
trying with the little strength remaining
to sputter "Drop and give me twenty"
to the nursing home attendant.
Drop. Sputter.
Drop. Sputter.
Drop and give me.
Sputter.
Twenty.

Thank you."

There was a smattering of applause, and Dustin jumped off the stage and came back to the table.

"One of your better efforts," said Anna. Beatnik poetry suited Dustin pretty well.

"Thanks," said Dustin. "Think it'll convince Coach Hunter to kill himself?"

"I doubt it," said Brian. "I'm not really sure he can read anything other than football playbooks."

"That's a good point," said James. "Maybe we should write up a depressing playbook or something."

I tried to imagine a playbook that said something like "27 pass the ball to 12. 12 start running, and just keep running and running, because everything is pointless anyway."

We sat there and drank our coffee. I kept my coat on so Anna couldn't see what a good job she'd done giving me the hickey—I was afraid that would just make her want to give me another one on the other side of my neck. Still, her foot was brushing against mine, and I was pretty sure she was doing it on purpose.

Meanwhile, Brian and Edie were up to their usual routine of making Bambi eyes at each other, and Edie occasionally sucked on Brian's fingers like they were pacifiers or something. It was disgusting, but it kept her from talking, which could occasionally be a blessing.

Finally, Brian withdrew his hand from Edie's mouth to look at his watch. "It's probably about halftime," he said. "You guys want to head out of here?"

"What for?" Anna asked.

"I feel like getting a burger," he said. "A cheap one."

"We'll probably have to go up to Cedar Avenue to get a cheap one," I said. "It's quite a walk."

"It's only a couple blocks farther than the high school."

Edie made a nasty face. We all generally preferred Sip

and the places that were left in the triangle to the retail wasteland on Cedar Avenue, but Edie hated even to set foot on that street.

"Do we have to?" she asked.

"You won't die," said Anna. "It's not like you'll disintegrate the minute you step into a Burger Box parking lot."

"I might," she insisted.

"You won't," said Anna. "The government stopped setting booby traps to catch communists in fast-food parking lots when the Berlin Wall fell."

"C'mon," said Brian. "Pretty please?"

Brian was a cool guy. Clearly, any man who is into both mechanical things and fire is destined to do great things in life. But if there's anything more disturbing than seeing your dad with a Mohawk, it's seeing a pyro saying "pretty please."

Edie rolled her eyes and said "Whatever," and we dropped our money off on the table. James and Dustin stayed behind; Dustin was busy scribbling another poem on a napkin, and James was busily looking over his shoulder.

We headed out into the cold and started walking back north, toward the high school. The wind had picked up a bit since we'd been in the coffee shop, and now it felt like an arctic wasteland outside. I felt like we were trekking through the frozen wilderness toward Shangri-la or something, except that the destination was not a tropical paradise—it was probably going to be a gas station that sold cheap frozen burgers.

Brian and Edie clung to each other really tightly, kissing frequently, and for a moment I worried that their lips might stick together, the way your tongue can stick to metal when it's really cold out. But they seemed to be able to separate pretty well.

Anna, meanwhile, had her arm wrapped around mine, and I couldn't be sure whether it was a display of affection or just an attempt to stay warm, but I decided to consider it the former.

Cedar Avenue was a few blocks past the high school. When I was a little kid, it was a mostly empty road that you took to get to the mall or the interstate, but over the last few years, it was as though someone had planted strip mall seeds around it, and practically overnight, it had turned into the new downtown. Even the stores inside the old mall were starting to close down.

The road was lined with giant signs that shed light all over the place, making the snow on the ground glow red, blue, and yellow. The giant blue Mega Mart sign at the end of the street stared down as if it were surveying the whole scene; if it had eyes, it could probably even see the skeletons of the stores on Venture Street that had closed down after the Mega Mart opened. If the noise from the traffic died down, I'll bet you could hear that sign laughing.

Good ol' Comrade Edie made no bones about the fact that she thought the whole street was disgusting.

"Being on this street," she said, "is like being in a commercial for something I don't want."

"Yeah," said Brian, "but where else are you going to go for a cheap burger at this time of night?"

"C'mon," I said. "I'm pretty sure the Quickway lets communists in. Their sign is red." Don't ask me why, but communists tend to be attracted to things that are red. If anyone makes a public television nature documentary about suburban commies, they'll have to mention that.

Inside the Quickway, Brian immediately headed for the slushee machine and started to pour himself an enormous one.

"Jesus, Brian," said Edie. "How big a slushee do you need?"

"Well, what the hell am I supposed to do?" he asked. "It only costs a dime to upgrade to the 'holy crap' size. You can't pass that up."

"Sure you can," she said.

"Yeah," said Brian, "but I wouldn't want it on my conscience."

He took his slushee, which was roughly the size of a barrel, to the cooler, where there were a bunch of plastic-wrapped one-dollar sandwiches and a little microwave for heating them up. I picked out a turkey sandwich on honey wheat bread with caramelized onions, Anna got a BLT, and Brian and Edie both got cheeseburgers—Edie may not have wanted to be there, but I guess commies have to eat, too.

"All they have are cheeseburgers," she whined. "Why can't they have any without the damn cheese?" She took the burger out of the plastic wrap and took out the slice of American cheese, putting it in her pocket before she put the burger in the microwave.

As Brian and Edie took their stuff out to the parking lot to eat, Anna and I took turns with the microwave.

"Edie's sort of a whiner, isn't she?" I asked.

"I guess so," said Anna. "But my dad hates this street, too. He says it makes the town look like the airport."

"I think so, too," I said, though I'd never really stopped

to think about it. I didn't want to seem like some kind of copycat, but Anna and her dad were pretty good at convincing me of pretty much anything. If anyone else, like, say, my parents, had told me I should build up to drinking my coffee black, I would have thought they were insane.

We joined Brian and Edie in the parking lot and stood around eating our food, watching the cars drive in and out. My sandwich wasn't half bad; turkey, honey wheat, and caramelized onions had sounded suspiciously fancy for a gas-station sandwich, and I questioned how they could use safe ingredients, keep them fresh, and still be able to sell the thing for a buck, but it tasted all right, and it didn't glow in the dark or anything, as far as I could tell. The sky was dark, but there were so many lights going that I probably couldn't have told if the thing was glowing. Maybe that's the idea behind having gas stations well lit.

The night air was thick with the smell of French fries and dirty snow. Near the door, somebody had written the word "SHIT" on one of the bricks with Wite-Out, presumably protesting something or other.

After a few minutes, we started heading back in the general direction of the high school, since we'd have to get back in enough time to warm back up. If my dad picked me up and I looked like I'd been out in the cold all night, I'd be in big trouble.

Once we got past the Burger Box, on Seventy-first and Venture, the green sign for Wackfords Coffee came into view, and Brian called out "Wackfords!" and socked me in the arm. I would have been pissed off if I weren't well familiar with the rules of the Wackfords game—when you see a Wackfords, you shout "Wackfords!" and whack the person next to you in the arm. You can really get hurt playing it in the city, where there's one on every corner.

We were about the last town in the state to get a Wackfords, and Edie, naturally, was pissed that they had come to town at all. The only person I knew who'd actually been inside was Dustin, who'd gone there once to try to arrange a poetry reading and had been told that they never did things like that. They tried to act like a cool coffee shop, like Sip, but for all I could tell, they were really just another fast-food joint. They made the employees wear uniforms and everything.

Edie stood in front of the Wackfords sign when we got closer to it. It looked like she was having a staring contest with it. The green light covered her entire body and made her look sort of like an alien in a bad sci-fi movie from the 1950s.

"You suck!" she screamed at the sign. Anna and I couldn't help laughing at her.

"Yeah, man!" said Brian.

"It's not even a coffee shop," said Edie. "It's just an office!"

"Yeah," said Brian. "An office!"

Edie pulled the slice of American cheese out of her pocket, tore it in half, and threw one of the halves directly at the sign. It hit it square on the "R," stuck there for a second, then fell to the ground.

Suddenly, a head poked out from the door. It was a young, curly-headed guy in a Wackfords apron.

"Aw, be nice," he said. He shut the door and disappeared back into the store just as Edie was throwing the other half of her cheese at him. It fell well short of the door, and I was glad she hadn't hit him. I doubted you could actually be arrested for assault with half a slice of American cheese, but it's best not to take your chances with things like that. Especially in towns where cops are expected to be busy chasing gangbangers but don't really have much to do.

We stood there in the parking lot for a minute, surrounded by signs that towered over us like giants. A few of the gas-station logos were reflected in Anna's glasses. I thought that maybe, someday in the future, another, newer downtown would pop up a mile or two north, and all these places would be empty shells of stores just like the ones that were starting to fill up Venture Street and the mall. All the signs would be like gravestones. I'd go up there with a can of spray paint and write "Here lies" above the names of the stores, if I was still in town, which I prayed I wouldn't be.

That night, after I got home, I stood at my window, looking at all of the different-colored lights in the sky. I could see a bunch of rooftops from the Flowers' Grove neighborhood a couple of blocks past mine, and, back behind those, quite a few of the lights from the signs on Cedar Avenue. Red from the Quickway. Yellow from the Burger Box. I couldn't see any of the blue Mega Mart sign, except for maybe a bit of a hazy blue glow, but right between two rooftops a few blocks back, through some bare branches of the January trees, I could see just a little bit of the green from the Wackfords sign. I'd never noticed it before. It hadn't been there very long, after all.

Before I finally went to bed, I stared at that little green light for a long, long time.

On Saturday morning, I noticed a new bit of Magnetic Poetry on the fridge:

> Darling son
> light of your years
> please glow from our wisdom
> and keep certain parts
> behind closed pants
> until you grow into marriage.

I wished I had Dustin Eddlebeck's skill at writing poetry to put up a response. I was pretty sure I could write a better poem than that, but Magnetic Poetry has certain limitations. If they made tiles saying "go to hell, geezers," my mother would not have allowed them on the fridge in the first place.

That evening, I got a call from Dustin.

"Can you be at Sip at about seven?" he asked. "Anna's called a summit meeting."

"She did?" I asked. "Why didn't she tell me herself?"

"Summit meeting, man. It's protocol."

Summit meetings, when the gifted pool got together to plot some form of strategy, were rare—we'd only had one of them before, about a month after *La Dolce Pubert* was finished, when we'd plotted ways to make sure every kid in school could see it. The protocol for summit meetings was that Anna would be notified first (unless it was her idea, which it had been both times now); then she'd call Brian, whose last name was after hers in alphabetical order. He'd call Marcus Clinch, and Marcus would call James Cole, and James would call Dustin Eddlebeck, who would then call me. My job would be to call Jenny Kurosawa, whose name came after "Harris" on the list.

"Okay," I said. "I'll see what I can do."

As usual, Jenny's parents gave me a regular interrogation as to why I wanted to talk to their daughter—if it wasn't school related, they probably would have hung up on me. I was sure she'd never told them about my getting suspended over a movie for which she herself had helped with the music. If she had, they probably would have blocked my number. I had to make up stories about algebra questions for a good five minutes, but that was easy enough—I didn't have to be much of an actor to convince people that I didn't understand polynomials. Finally, they let her on the phone.

"Hi, Leon!" she said, sounding awfully excited just to get a phone call.

"Summit meeting," I said. "Tonight at seven o'clock, Sip Coffee in the triangle."

She paused. "I'm not sure I can get there," she said. "They'll never let me out for that."

"Well, make it if you can," I said. She said she'd try.

I ran downstairs and asked my dad if I could get a ride to the coffee shop at seven.

"Well," he said, "we were going to be eating around that time, Leon."

"What are we having?"

"I don't know. Probably something from the grilling book."

This, of course, called for fast strategy.

"Would it be all right if I just ate at Sip? They have pretty good sandwiches there, and I have to meet some people to work on a project."

"Well, as long as it's for school," he said. "I'll drive you."

I was the first to arrive at Sip; Dad took me a bit early so he and my mother could have whatever hideous crap they were planning to eat before all their TV shows came on. Jenny walked in a minute after me, wearing one of her Doors shirts over what looked like about three layers of sweaters, and decked out in gloves, a hat, a scarf, and earmuffs—the whole winter set.

"You made it!" I said.

"Yeah," she said, taking off her gloves and putting her "Jim Morrison's Soul" bottle on the table. "If my parents ever ask, I'm running sprints to try out for track."

"In the middle of January?"

She smiled. "According to the latest studies," she said, suddenly speaking like the narrator of a PBS documentary about athletes, "wintry nights provide the ideal atmosphere for physical conditioning."

"Nice."

"Anyway, do you know what the meeting is about?"

"No clue," I said. "I know it was Anna's idea, but I didn't call to ask. There's protocol to follow."

I don't know why we were so formal about summit meetings. It was probably just more fun that way.

Having set all her stuff down, Jenny climbed up and stood on top of the table.

"All hail the American night!" she shouted at the ceiling. I assumed this was something Jim Morrison used to say. Apparently, part of being an obsessed Doors fan is trying to live on the edge, and to her, standing on a table was really pushing some limits. Had there been anyone in the café besides us and Trinity, I'm sure they would have stared.

"Hey!" shouted Trinity. "Get down!"

Jenny just looked over at her with a face like she was on a roller coaster. I'd never seen her so excited.

"I made the blue cars go away!" she shouted down at Trinity.

"Yeah," said Trinity. "But there's a ceiling fan right by you. Get down before it takes your head off."

"Oh," said Jenny, a bit sheepishly. She jumped down and took a seat.

"Living on the edge these days, huh?" I asked.

She smiled. "Just being out at night like this . . . it's like I'm busting out of jail, you know? I mean, my parents might disown me for this! It's so exciting!"

One by one, most of the rest of the group started to file

in. Dustin and Brian came in at pretty much the same time, and Edie showed up a minute later. Most of the rest of the people weren't as likely to show. Everyone in the pool could be counted on to do something that would raise eyebrows for our projects, and we could all be trusted to raise a little hell in the classrooms from time to time. But some of the other kids just didn't get out of the house much, or were always busy with real extracurricular junk. Those of us who came to things like summit meetings were the ones who wouldn't be caught dead joining the Spanish club—or, in Jenny's case, would join but were always on the lookout for an excuse to miss the meetings.

Anna was the last to arrive, and she sat down in the seat I'd quietly saved for her by piling my coat and bag on the chair next to me.

"Good evening," she said, sounding very formal. "Welcome to the summit meeting."

Before we could get started, Trinity walked, or rather, danced her way over to the table.

"Wow, the gang's all here," she said. "What are you guys? Like, the Cornersville weirdo club or something?"

"Gifted pool," said Dustin, chuckling. "Same thing."

"Oh," said Trinity, as though we suddenly made a lot more sense to her. "I was in the gifted pool in middle school. It was the weirdo club then, too!"

"Cheers, comrade," said Edie, raising an empty coffee mug that had been sitting on the table.

"Yeah, whatever," said Trinity. "You guys want coffee or what?"

We all ordered cups. Jenny ordered a cup with two shots

40

of espresso in it, which to her was probably the equivalent of ordering speed. Trinity brought them out a minute later on a tray. "I must be insane," she said. "Bringing caffeine to a bunch of eighth graders."

"And eighth grade ne'er-do-wells, at that," I reminded her.

"All right," said Anna as Trinity danced her way back to the counter. "I hereby call this summit meeting to order."

"Great," said Brian. "What's it all about?"

"I have an idea for the next movie project," she said. I leaned in closer. We all knew that if the next movie didn't make a really big splash, no one would watch anything else we did. *The Rooster in the Skating Rink* had been our sophomore slump, and now we needed a real homer.

"Something else avant-garde?" asked Jenny.

"Not exactly," Anna said. "I was thinking of a sort of documentary."

"About what?" I asked.

"The old downtown and Cedar Avenue."

"What about them?" Edie asked. "About how all those capitalist pigs exploit their workers?"

"Something like that," said Anna. "I was mostly thinking about how you said Wackfords was more of an office than a coffee shop last night."

"Yeah?" Edie asked.

"I was thinking we could do a short documentary contrasting the style and substance of the old downtown versus the faceless corporate garbage of the new strip malls."

"Or better yet," said Edie slowly, as though she was choosing her words carefully for once, "we could take over the Mega Mart."

Nobody seemed to take this seriously. What were we going to do—charge in and take the place over at gunpoint, then steal ourselves a couple of cheap shirts?

But Anna nodded, considering the suggestion from the floor. "That's an interesting concept," she said. "Go on."

"We'll take it over like pirates," said Edie, grinning.

"Avast!" shouted Brian, in his best pirate accent. The rest of us joined in with a chorus of "arrrr's."

"I don't know," said Anna, even though she was smiling. "That sounds just slightly illegal. It's not worth going to jail over."

"Jail?" asked Jenny. She had been leaning in close, but now she pulled away a bit. If being in a café under legal pretenses was risky to her, I could only imagine how far out of her league it was to even joke about something that could lead to jail time.

"Then we'll do it at Wackfords," said Edie. "They're way smaller, so they'd be easy to take over. Then we'll turn it into an accounting office or something and see if anyone even notices!"

"Maybe," said Anna, laughing, "we can find a way to set up an office in the Wackfords without actually doing anything illegal."

"Yeah," I said. "If we showed up with a watercooler and some ferns and set them up in the middle of the store and started handing out paperwork or something, nobody would even notice the difference. We could probably film a pretty good scene. And the most they could do is ask us to move."

"I could see that working out," said Anna.

"Well," said Edie, "I suppose that might work. It would be better if we could tell customers they didn't sell coffee anymore, though, because it's just an office now."

"Anyway," said Anna, "the point of the movie will be to make a monument to the old downtown, so we can use it as our pool project, and point out that Cedar Avenue sucks, however we go about it. And maybe we can have a scene showing a full accounting office being set up in Wackfords and not having anyone even notice. Everybody in?"

"You know I am," I said. "We could maybe even prove an actual point with this one."

"I'm in," said Edie. "So's Brian."

Right about then, we heard Trinity squeal, and she ran to the front door, where a curly-headed guy had just walked in the door.

"Troy!" she shouted. She jumped over the counter and leapt up at him. For a second I thought she was going to knock him down, but he caught her and held her up by the butt while she wrapped her arms and legs around him. I hoped, for his sake, that all the safety pins on her dress were securely fastened. The guy—what I could see of him through Trinity—looked vaguely familiar, though I couldn't quite put my finger on why.

She jumped down after a second, then said, "Troy, come here, you have to meet these kids." She grabbed his hand and practically dragged him over to our table. "Check it out," she said, pointing at us. "These are the kids who are in the gifted pool this year." She turned to us. "Troy was in it the same time I was."

"I know you," said Troy, grinning at Edie.

"You do?" asked Edie, looking confused.

"Yeah," said Troy. "You threw a piece of cheese at me last night."

That was why he looked familiar.

He worked at Wackfords.

"Corporate whore!" Edie spat with a sneer.

Troy chuckled. "I just work there, you know," he said. "It's not like I have some vested interest in the company or anything."

"Oh, come on," said Edie. "No one *has* to work there."

"No," said Troy, "I could always go work at the Mega Mart up the street instead. Or at one of the fast-food places. Nobody outside of Cedar Avenue is hiring these days, and you gotta work someplace."

"But someplace like *that?*" Edie asked.

"Hey," Troy explained, "Andy, this one guy I work with, says that retail is, like, the modern equivalent of going to work in the mines. At least I'm in one of the nice, well-lit mines that doesn't smell too bad. I could even get insurance if they gave me enough hours. Plus, if I die in a cave-in or something, they'd probably alert the proper authorities. Mega Mart would have my clothes up on the rack before I was cold."

"Why didn't you just get a job here?" asked Brian.

Troy laughed again. "You don't get that lucky," he said.

"Trinity did," said Edie.

"That wasn't luck," Trinity interrupted.

"She had to sleep with, like, five people to get this job," Troy said. Trinity socked him in the arm. Hard.

"I did not," she said, while Troy rubbed his arm and mouthed the words "She did." "I was bagging groceries for a year and a half while I waited for an opening here. And it was a pay cut."

"Hmmm," said Edie, clearly not convinced.

"Look," said Troy. "Would you like me better if I told you I was bringing the place down from the inside by not working very hard?"

"Well," Edie said, "I guess so. In a way."

"You know, Troy," I said, "we were just talking about Wackfords. Do you think anybody would notice if people set up an office in there?"

He shrugged. "Not really. Everyone acts like it's the office anyway. I've had people ask me to keep the noise down when the blender was running so they could talk on their phones."

"Edie wants us to take them over like pirates," said Jenny, "but we think that might be a little bit extreme."

"Might be a little bit illegal, too," said Troy.

"Just let them try to stop us," Edie muttered.

"Actually," I said, "we were thinking of filming a scene where we set up a regular accounting office in there, just to see if anyone even really notices. We could probably do it without getting in your way at all."

"That might be kind of cool," said Troy. "I can maybe

46

help you pick times to come in when it's just me and Andy working. I know he'd look the other way and let you guys do what you gotta do. Even if you don't do the takeover thing, you should at least come and talk to Andy. He's a McHobo."

"What's a McHobo?" I asked.

"As I understand it, it's anyone who bums from job to job and never stays anywhere long enough to specialize. But he gets really philosophical about it. You could probably make a whole movie just about him."

The music over the speaker suddenly changed from a waltz (I think) to something that sounded like a tango, and Trinity said, "Troy! Dance!" and pulled him up from the chair where he'd been sitting, then proceeded to lead him around the store, tango dancing. He looked like he was just following along as well as he could without falling on his ass, but he played along like a good sport.

"We are *so* learning how to do that, Brian," said Edie.

Brian kind of shrugged sheepishly.

"Well," Anna said as Troy and Trinity danced farther and farther away, "I'd probably better get going in a minute."

"Me too," said Jenny.

So everybody began packing up. I hung around Anna as she bundled up. She'd be walking home, even though it was still hellishly cold out. She lived right near the triangle, which I don't think was coincidence. I could imagine her parents wanting a place near the old downtown—if they had to live in suburbia, they probably figured they might as well choose the best location they could find under the circumstances.

"That was a really good idea," I said. "I think this'll make a great movie. Even if we don't stage a corporate takeover."

47

Anna chuckled. "Edie's weird, that's all," she said. "There's this fine line between being an activist and just mouthing off, and she wouldn't know it if it marched down Venture Street at the head of an oompah band."

"Ha," I said. I leaned in and kissed her, just on the cheek, which I figured was pretty safe. She didn't stop me or anything, though she also didn't kiss me back, I noticed. And it bugged me.

"Nighty night," she said, and I think she might have been trying to say it really sexily on purpose. Sometimes I just couldn't tell. It certainly sounded sexy to me, but she could have been talking about cleaning her cat's litter box and I probably would have thought she sounded sexy.

She smiled and took off down the road.

I decided to stick around a little while to make sure I missed the evening's grilling adventure. Trinity and Troy were still dancing around—or anyway, Troy was hanging on to Trinity while she danced around. Pretty soon Troy was just sort of standing there while Trinity danced around him—all around him. There were times when it looked like she was rubbing her entire body against his; then her leg would wrap around him and she'd be rubbing specific parts of herself against him. I made up my mind right away that Anna and I were *so* learning to do that, too.

Then George, the owner, came out of the back room carrying a bag of coffee beans. George was a good guy—he was in his forties or so, had a scraggly brown beard, and wore a straw cowboy hat. When he was the only one working, the music tended to be acoustic classic rock—the Eagles, James Taylor, early Elton John, Grateful Dead, and whatnot.

"Hey, George," said Trinity, pausing from dancing at a point when her crotch was pressed right into Troy's side.

"Consorting with the enemy, eh, Trin?" George asked.

"If that's what you want to call it, sir," said Troy.

Trinity pried herself off Troy and smoothed her dress. "I'm prying corporate secrets out of him the old-fashioned way," she explained.

"Well, do what you have to do," said George. "Whatever it takes to keep us from going out of business around here."

"Can we do it on the counter?" asked Trinity.

"Whatever."

"How about in the back, by the ice machine?"

"Hey," said Troy, "I didn't agree to any of this."

"You'll do as you're told," said Trinity cutely.

"Six months," said George to Troy. "Six months and we shut down. I'll probably have to go on welfare and live in a box by next Christmas. Tell your manager."

What?

"Yeah," said Trinity. "So get back there, clean up the area around the ice machine, and take off your clothes. Move it!"

She pushed him in the chest in the general direction of the back room.

"Excuse me?" said some woman at the counter. "Can I get some service here?"

"One second," said Trinity, walking back over to the counter. "You!" She pointed at Troy. "Back there and strip. Now!"

Troy just stood there for a second, grinning.

"Move!" she said more forcefully as she got behind the counter.

Troy headed for the back room.

George snickered. "You crazy kids," he said.

"We're seriously gonna do it, George," said Trinity. "The things I do to save this store from the Wackfords!"

"I appreciate it, Trin," said George. "I really do."

I wasn't sure which I had to process first—the fact that Trinity was acting so randy at work and getting away with it, or that George had said Sip was closing in six months.

I looked around the place and didn't see any going out of business signs, but there was also nobody else there, other than Jenny and the woman standing at the counter. Business wasn't exactly booming. The tip jar on the counter looked pretty vacant. And six months is a bit early to put up going out of business signs.

Maybe it was true. It made perfect sense—everything else in the old downtown was dying, after all, and Wackfords was surely sucking up most of what coffee business existed in town. George wasn't acting like he was kidding.

Those bastards.

I wandered out of the store, ready to call for a ride, feeling a sort of a throbbing in my head. Sip was about the last good thing left in town. If it was gone, there'd be nowhere for Dustin to read his poems. I mean, we could always go to Fat Johnny's instead, but they didn't serve coffee, there was no open mike, and I doubted that they'd be around long, either. The only time you ever saw anyone there was after the high school football games, and if another pizza place opened closer to the high school, they'd be toast.

Pretty soon the old downtown, and the neighborhoods where Anna and I lived, would just be old houses in the middle of a wasteland of strip malls and new subdivisions without any sidewalks, streets that didn't go anywhere, and one white house after another. The local papers were talking about the town like it was suddenly being born, but none of them seemed to notice that it was actually dying.

Until the week before, I'd never really been bothered by it, but suddenly, just thinking about the new downtown was giving me a serious headache.

I was just about to call my parents for a ride when Jenny showed up outside, breaking my train of thought.

"Hey, Leon," she said.

"Hey," I said. "You got a ride coming?"

She shook her head. "I'm supposed to be out running wind sprints in the neighborhood," she said. "If I call asking for a ride from here, I'll be dead meat."

"Where do you live?" I asked.

She pointed down the road. "Way out in Oak Meadow Mills," she said. "I started walking right after you called me."

Oak Meadow Mills was one of the new subdivisions off of the highway. It wasn't really walking distance to anything.

"Jesus," I said. "You're gonna freeze to death if you try walking clear back there now."

For a second I thought I should offer to get her a ride with my parents, but then I remembered that it wouldn't be my mother and father picking me up, it would be Lester and Wanda: Grilling Americans. I certainly didn't want her to see them like that.

"Wanna split a cab or something?" I asked, thinking as quickly as I could. I could probably afford to share one, I figured, though I really didn't have any idea what it cost to take a cab. The rule was that I had to call for a ride. It didn't really specify *who* I was supposed to call.

"A taxi?" she said. "Do they have those around here?"

"I think you can get one if you call a cab company or something," I said. "It'll probably cost a few bucks, but we can split it."

"I'll pay for both of us!" she said quickly. "I have cash."

"You don't have to do that," I said. "I'll get my share."

"No," she said. "I insist. I'm loaded. I get allowance, but I'm never allowed to spend it on anything."

"Well," I said, "if you say so." I was never one to turn down free money, after all.

I pulled out my phone, dialed information, and asked to be connected with a cab company in Cornersville Trace. There was only one of them, but they put me right through to a guy who said someone could be at the triangle in ten minutes.

"This is so cool!" Jenny said. She was actually bouncing up and down, though it might have been just in an attempt to stay warm or the effect of all the espresso. "I mean, I thought only people in places like New York and Chicago took cabs."

"My parents are gonna freak out," I said. "I'm supposed to call them for a ride, but technically, there's no rule saying I can't get a cab."

She laughed and jumped some more. It was a good prank for me and all, but it was really living on the edge for her.

"That is so awesome," she said. "I mean, you always have the best ideas. That movie you made last semester was so cool, and then there were riots and stuff. . . . I'll bet it's the kind of stuff Jim Morrison did when he was in eighth grade."

"Well, I don't know about that," I said. "They weren't really riots, exactly, just, like, gatherings. And they were mostly over in five minutes." It's hard to stage a proper riot when most people have to catch a bus home.

"Still," she said. "I just, like, totally admire people who can do things like that. That's how people should live, like, taking risks, pushing the boundaries of reality, and things like that."

I'd never thought of the movie as pushing the boundaries of reality—pushing the boundaries of what you could do in a school sex-ed film, maybe, but not reality. This is not to say that I minded praise or anything.

"Are you going to do the new movie with us?" I asked.

She smiled again but kinda did this thing where she half rolled her eyes. "I don't know," she said. "I mean, I'll help any way I can, but if you guys end up taking over the Mega Mart, there's no way. My parents would chain me to a wall in the basement until I turn eighteen if they found out I was involved in something like that. Or send me to military school."

"That's just Edie talking," I said. "There's no way we can take over the Mega Mart."

Just then, it occurred to me that the thing about taking over the Wackfords might be an even better idea than I thought—and not just setting up an office there, like Anna suggested, but taking it over like pirates, like Edie wanted to. If Trinity could still save Sip with some strategic sexual escapades, taking over the Wackfords probably couldn't hurt, either. This was certainly something to consider.

Jenny walked over to the fire hydrant and ran her finger over the top of it, I guess to see if it was covered with ice or something.

"Careful," I said. "You know what dogs do to those things!"

With one foot, she stepped up onto the top of the hydrant and stood on it, lifting her other foot into the air and howling at the moon. Trying to set the night on fire, I suppose. I don't think I'd ever seen anybody having such a good time just standing around outside a coffee shop, but in a way, I knew where she was coming from. There was a certain thrill just to being out on the streets, after dark, without any parents—mine or anyone else's—around. I was getting kind of used to it, but my parents weren't overprotective in the slightest compared to Jenny's.

A minute later the cab pulled up. It didn't look like a cab to me. I always pictured the yellow things with the black and white checks on the side, but this just looked like a little maroon sedan that said "Bonaventure Taxi Service" in white letters on the door. It looked sort of dingy. But it had the light-up thing on top like cabs always have on TV, which was good enough for me.

I opened the back door, and Jenny climbed in, and I got in after her.

"Where to?" said the guy driving the cab.

"Uh, 7942 August Avenue, please," I said.

"And from there to Oak Meadow Mills," said Jenny.

"Sure," said the guy.

And he took off.

The driver had sort of a shag mullet and a mustache, as though he had found a look he liked in 1978 and had just stuck with it ever since. He had clearly been blond at one point, though his hair was mostly gray now. His fingers drummed on the dashboard, keeping the rhythm to a classic rock song on the radio.

"Any objection to Led Zeppelin?" he asked.

"Not at all," I said.

"Good." He turned the stereo up a bit and drummed harder. I got the idea that this was how he'd spent every night of the last few decades—driving around, drumming along to classic rock. Not a bad life, really.

I took a quick whiff of the air. I'd always heard that taxi drivers were known for not bathing, but this one smelled like a mixture of cigarettes and air freshener, which, together, smelled like a forest full of old people—nothing *too* offensive.

We got about a block before Jenny looked over at me, smiling so wide I could only assume that she'd be sore in the morning. "This was a great idea, Leon. Thanks."

"Hey, thanks for the fare," I said.

"You know," she said, suddenly smiling a bit less, "I'm not really sure I understand what's going on with you and Anna."

She had taken off her hat and was kind of playing with her hair.

"Well," I said, "it's complicated, I guess. One of those things."

"Yeah," she said. "Like sometimes I think you're a couple, and sometimes I think you're just friends."

"Yeah," I said. "It's somewhere in between, I guess."

"Okay," she said.

And she turned to look out of her window, still playing with her hair, wrapping it around her finger, then unwinding it and starting over.

I looked up at the cabdriver, eager to change the subject.

"Have you been driving a cab long?" I asked. I always saw guys in movies asking that.

"Oh, hell yeah," he said. "Nineteen years now. Hey, you guys mind if I smoke a bit?"

"Go ahead!" said Jenny. He opened up the glove compartment and pulled out a pack of smokes and a lighter.

"Have you been driving in Cornersville all that time?" I asked.

"Hell no!" he said. "Nineteen years ago there wouldn't have been nobody to drive in Cornersville. I still don't come out here much, on account of the cops out here are insane, but it's easier work than in the city, and some nights I just wanna rock, ya know?"

"Hell yeah," said Jenny.

"Until a few years ago you never got nobody out here. It was just a little, you know." And he made a weird noise like a duck having sex, which I guess meant that until a few years ago, the town was just a little place where ducks got it on.

"The town's gotten a lot bigger, hasn't it?" I asked.

"Well," he said, "that's what happens when you build a town near a city, man. I remember when I first started all this, people thought that Shaker Heights was just a little crap town out in the middle of nowhere."

Shaker Heights was the next town between Cornersville and the city. The two towns were creeping closer and closer together; I figured that in a few years, there'd be no space between them, just a big field of subdivisions connecting the borders like stitches.

"And Preston will be next," Jenny said. Preston was a

small town, quite a bit smaller than Cornersville, about five miles north, past a long stretch of farmland.

"Oh, just watch," said the guy. "In ten years there won't be any space left between Cornersville and Preston. Some developer's gonna buy up those farms, and that whole area's gonna explode like shit. Just watch."

I kind of got a kick out of the fact that the driver was cursing and smoking in front of us. Most adults seem to be under the impression that people my age don't know what all the cusswords are. Still, I wasn't sure I liked the image of anything exploding like shit. Ew.

About this time he pulled up to my house, rolled down the window a crack, and blew some smoke out into the air.

"I'll get all the fare when we get to my place," said Jenny.

"This where you get off, then?" the cabbie asked me.

"Yeah," I said. "Thanks." I looked over at Jenny. "And thank you, too!"

Jenny smiled. I smiled back, and was just about to climb out, but I was totally unprepared for what happened next: she leaned in closer and kissed me. Not quite on the lips or anything, it was on that little corner between the mouth and the cheek, like maybe she'd been going for one or the other but ended up in between.

"Good night," she said.

"Uh, yeah," I said. "Good night."

I practically jumped out of the car and shut the door, then ran around the front of it and into my driveway.

"Thanks for the ride," I said to the cabdriver.

"Rock on, my good man," he said.

"Rock on," I said, making the devil sign with my hand. She kissed me. Jenny.

And there was a fifty-fifty chance she had intended to kiss me on the lips.

I stood there in the driveway sort of blindsided for a second as the cab pulled away, drove up August Avenue, and turned onto Eighty-second Street.

Okay, I thought. So she kissed me. It's probably just a part of her whole "living on the edge" thing. Maybe she read that Jim Morrison kissed people all the time just as a way of saying good-bye. That was probably it. It had to be.

But then I remembered her asking what my deal with Anna was. But I hadn't told her it was nothing, or anything like that. I'd said we were sort of in between. Surely she hadn't seen that as a license to start going after me herself, right?

I sort of stood there in the cold for a second, letting the snow hit my face, while I tried to shake the feeling that I'd just cheated on Anna. Jenny had kissed me, not the other way around, and anyway, Anna and I weren't really an official couple or anything. No rule said no one else could kiss me.

For the first time that night, I really felt cold.

I only had time to think about this for a second or so, though, before I heard my mother shouting at me.

"Leon!" she shouted. "Get in here this instant!"

I turned around and headed up to the front door, where she was standing, still wearing her Wanda gear.

"What the heck is going on here? Was that a police car?"

I laughed. "No. Jenny and I called a cab."

"A *cab?*" she asked, as though I'd said it was a carriage

made of a pumpkin or something equally unlikely. "Leon, you know you're supposed to call us for a ride!"

"Aha!" I said. "The rule is that I'm supposed to call for a ride. There's no rule about *who* I have to call."

My dad showed up behind her, still wearing his Lester hat. "What's going on?" he asked.

"Your son," said my mother, "just came home from the café in a taxicab."

"No kidding?" asked my dad. "What did that cost you?"

"Not much," I said, not wanting to say that I'd let someone else pay.

"Well, that was an okay idea," said my dad. "But it would have been cheaper just to call us."

"Yeah," I said, "I was going to. But Jenny was going to be stuck walking clear back to Oak Meadow Mills, and it's freezing outside, so I offered to split a cab with her."

"Well, that was nice of you, I guess," he said.

"Yeah, it was just a favor for a friend, that's all," I said. "I would have done it for any of my friends." It wasn't like I had ridden with Jenny because I had a thing for her or anything. I was telling myself as much as I was telling them.

"Well," said my mother, "I think that's all beside the point. You know that when we say you're to call for a ride, we mean to call us, not a cab. We would have given Jenny a ride home."

"It might have been implied," I said, "but it was never explicit."

"Have you been reading legal thrillers or something?" asked my mother. "Because lawyer-speak isn't going to get you out of trouble."

"Oh, Judith, there's no harm done," said my father. "He beat the system. Good for him!"

I wasn't too surprised that my dad thought this was clever; he was a lot more lenient on matters like this than my mother. But I'd never heard him say it was good to beat the system. Maybe that hair dye he'd used on the Mohawk had seeped into his brain.

"Well," said my mother again, "in the future, let it be known that you're to call *us*, not a taxi, a bus, a hansom cab, a volunteer service for drunks, a stolen Soviet tank, or Air Force One. And even if you just get a ride home from Anna's dad or something, call and let us know."

"Deal," I said.

My mother nodded and I headed up to my room, forgetting all about my parents and thinking about Jenny again. I couldn't think of any way I'd led her on, but I still felt guilty. But I reminded myself that it wasn't really that big of a deal or anything. She was just trying, in her way, to live on the edge a bit, like Jim Morrison. Kissing me was her way of pushing the bounds of reality.

Then again, it did seem like I spent every gifted-pool meeting with her butt on one of my arms. Maybe it wasn't an accident.

About twenty minutes later, I got an e-mail from Jenny. The subject line read "Plutonian Night."

```
Leon,
    Wasn't that cabdriver awesome? On the way
to my place he was singing along to the ra-
dio really loud, and he said the f-word
```

twice. Hope I didn't freak you out tonight
at the end of the cab ride. I couldn't help
myself. I know you and Anna are sort of going out and all, but if that ever changes, I
imagine you can guess that I'm interested.
Ever since I started reading biographies of
Jim Morrison I've wanted to live more on the
edge, cause some more trouble, and, you
know, actually live a bit instead of just
doing homework all the time. And the only
person I know who is actually doing that
sort of thing is you. And I'm not going to go
trying to split you and Anna up or anything,
but I just thought you should know that I
think you're awesome. I hope this doesn't
weird you out or anything, and that things
can still be the same between us as they've
always been if you aren't interested.
Sincerely,
Jenny

Whoa.

Well, that threw a bit of a wrench in my gears. No one
had ever written me a letter telling me how great I was.

I took a deep breath and thought about things.
Sometimes I felt like Anna and I were sort of stuck in neutral or something like that, and I always felt like maybe I
couldn't keep up with her. I mean, she was about ten times
smarter than I was, and despite the whole suspension thing,
I didn't think of myself as particularly rebellious. I mean,

even Anna wasn't all that rebellious—she was just better at living on her own terms than the rest of us. I imagine she probably would have been able to talk her way out of suspension if her movie had been the one Mrs. Smollet had a problem with. Anna and her parents were the kind of people I only hoped I could eventually be.

Maybe that was the way Jenny thought of me.

And I couldn't help being flattered.

I quickly wrote her a reply.

Jenny,

    Yeah, that cabdriver was all right. I've always heard that cabdrivers don't speak English and don't bathe. I'm not sure this guy bathed, exactly, but he certainly spoke English! Thanks again for the cab fare and the nice letter; I don't really think I'm as rebellious as all that, but I'm flattered that you think I am. Don't worry about things between us being weird—I'm sure they'll be the way they've always been. Not weird at all.
See ya,
Leon

I only wished I believed it.

5

With the exception of the time I spent staring out the window at the green light of the Wackfords sign, there wasn't a second on Saturday night or Sunday morning that I wasn't thinking about Anna or Jenny. Anna, mostly. When my thoughts turned to Jenny, I'd try to steer them over toward Anna. But I couldn't stop the things Jenny had written from running through my head. I thought—hell, I *knew*—that I should just call Anna and say, "Hey, what's the deal with us, anyway?" but when it comes to things like that, I'm a total chicken.

On Sunday afternoon, my dad offered to take me thrift-store shopping, and I readily agreed. I was not one to pass up a chance to hit the thrift stores, even with a guy with a Mohawk. And anything that would take my mind off of Jenny and Anna for a while was especially welcome.

When my parents went to the thrift stores together, it was usually on a cookbook hunt, but when my dad went alone, he was usually shopping for scientific gear—or, failing that, junk he could get away with calling scientific gear. Anything made out of glass was pretty much fair game; it didn't bother him in the slightest that real chemists probably don't keep their chemicals in bear-shaped honey containers or jars shaped like Santa Claus.

"I'm gonna need all the bowls I can get for this project," he said as we got into the car. "It'd be easier just to use the nonstick ones from the kitchen, but, well, you know." He snorted a bit. One of his least-favorite household rules was that he was not to use any of the kitchenware as lab equipment—he had to buy his own stuff for that. He tended to grumble about it, but it was one rule for which I thanked God daily.

"Hey," I said, "maybe you'll find something with Teflon at the thrift store."

"Ha!" He snorted again, and I wondered if maybe having the Mohawk was making him snottier. "Forget that. You never find anything that nice in the thrift-store cookware. It's mostly old, worn-out stuff. That's why I go through it so quickly out in the garage."

Well, that and the fact that he used them to mix hazardous chemicals that ate right through them. I thought this, but didn't say it.

"I'm out for records," I said.

"Naturally."

My old project had been buying large speakers, which come remarkably cheap at thrift stores and flea markets. I'd originally planned to buy enough to cover a whole wall in my room, but I'd stopped after I got about halfway, since the noise half a wall of sound made was already enough to break circuits, start fires, and generally cause trouble around the house. Once I'd declared that project kaput, I moved into buying actual records. I didn't own a record player or anything, but I needed something to decorate my other bedroom walls, the ones that weren't covered in speakers, and thrift-store records were way cheaper than actual posters.

I'd gotten the idea from Anna's parents' house. The walls in one of their hallways were lined with a bunch of framed jazz albums, which looked really cool and kind of elegant, in a way. It made me want to buy up old jazz albums and other artsy things like that to decorate my room, and that was my original plan, but I soon found that cool jazz records are a pretty rare find at thrift stores—they have records galore, but mostly Christmas albums, *Jane Fonda's Workout Record*, copies of that one album by Boston, and religious stuff. The closest thing you normally ever see to jazz is *Whipped Cream & Other Delights* by Herb Alpert and the Tijuana Brass, which I'm not sure really counts as jazz.

So, since the supply was much greater, I'd gotten into collecting albums with really stupid covers—which was not quite the same as cooking bad food on purpose, since I didn't actually listen to the albums. They just functioned as conversation pieces in the room, and anyway, I got a kick out of knowing that I was the only headbanger in town with an album on his wall called *Satan Is Real*, the cover of which featured a couple of preachers standing in front of what appeared to be a large cardboard devil that wasn't likely to convince anyone that Satan was, in fact, real. Also, I didn't really know all that much about jazz. Anyone who saw a bunch of jazz albums on the wall and questioned me about them would have realized I was a faker really fast.

An hour later, we were back in the car, heading home. Dad had found a whole bunch of bowls, a few wooden spoons, and, to his great delight, an old chemistry set.

"Look at this thing!" he said, practically bursting. "It's just like the ones I had when I was a kid . . . and most of the chemicals are still there!"

"Is it safe for them to sell it like that?" I asked.

"Nope," he said, smiling even wider. "Not in the slightest. The instructions are missing, and if you mix some of these together the wrong way, you could end up with stuff that would eat right through your skin, or cause something to blow up."

My stomach turned a little bit. This was the kind of speech that gave me nightmares. Every time I heard a loud noise in the garage—which was not uncommon—I'd worry that it might be "the big one." Even our cat acted like a shell-shocked veteran of World War I.

"Anyway," he said, "they're sure lucky I bought it, instead of some undesirable sort who's up to no good."

"Look at yourself, Dad," I said. "The lady at the counter probably thought *you* were an undesirable sort."

"Oh yeah." He chuckled. "I forgot that people tend to get scared of people with Mohawks. Well, let them think so. They have nothing to worry about. What did you get, anyway?"

"It was slim pickings today," I said. "Just this."

I held up a worn copy of something from the 1970s called *The Wildewood Singers Sing the Beatles*. It showed a bunch of middle-aged people standing in front of a tree, all of them looking as though they'd just robbed a hair-spray store and wanted to use up the evidence before the cops arrived. Dad made a nasty face at it.

"Leon," he said, "this thing looks awful. If you want to hear the Beatles, I have every one of their albums." For my dad, this was exhibiting pretty good taste. I'd always imagined he preferred bland choral versions of the Beatles' songs to the originals.

"You do?" I asked.

"Sure," he said. "Have you ever actually heard them before?"

"Of course," I said.

"Just checking," he said. "Lots of kids nowadays are surprised to hear that Paul McCartney had a band before Wings."

"Give me a break," I said. "That might have been funny in the seventies, but if there's a kid alive today who's never heard of the Beatles, there's no way that kid has heard of Wings."

"Fair enough," Dad nodded. "But seriously, throw that thing out the window. It looks like a travesty."

"Hey," I said. "I just got it for the cover; it's not like I'm going to listen to it. That would be like buying a book of nasty-looking recipes and then actually cooking them."

He paused. "Point taken," he said. I was a bit surprised by this; normally that's the kind of mouthing off that would get me in trouble. I guess having an armload of chemicals just put him in too good a mood.

We drove right past the Wackfords, but I refrained from whacking Dad in the arm. Cedar Avenue looked a lot different by day, when the signs weren't glowing.

"What do you think of all these new places?" I asked.

"Well," he said slowly, "the newspapers keep calling it the revival of Cornersville, like we were just a little dump before all the minimalls moved in. And I guess it's good for the economy. It creates a lot of jobs, having all these places."

"Not very good ones," I said. "They're mostly just name-tag jobs. I heard a guy last night saying that retail was sort of the modern equivalent of going to work in the mines."

He nodded. "That's probably about right. Most of the people who actually make any money off these places' being here live miles away in some fancy mansion, I suppose."

"So you don't like it?"

He shrugged one of his shoulders. "I like having some of the stores here, but on the whole, it's just making the town look more like every other town, and it makes the traffic a hell of a lot worse. So no, I guess I don't like it very much." He chuckled for a second. "Or maybe having a Mohawk just makes you automatically bored with the suburbs. Did they have any albums by the Sex Pistols back at the thrift store?"

"Hell no," I said.

"Rats," he said. "Ever since I got my new hairstyle, I've really felt like lashing out at society." He laughed again. I thoght maybe I should have Edie over—they could throw cheese at signs together.

"Warren doesn't like it much, either," I said. Warren was Anna's father.

"No," he said, "I don't suppose he would. How are you and Anna getting along?"

"Fine," I said, looking out the window. There were certain things I simply refused to discuss with my dad, but I knew he was ready to push the issue. I went for evasive ac-

68

tion. "Speaking of the gifted pool," I said, which we only sort of had been, "did I tell you about the new project we're doing?"

"Max Streich told me about it," he said. "Building monuments?"

"Yeah."

One of the main benefits of being in the gifted pool was that when my parents wanted to talk about school, I could just talk about whatever project we were working on for that until they were satisfied, and hence, I'd never have to bring up math, science, or any of the other subjects in which I could pretty confidently expect a C-plus, tops.

"What kind of monument are you thinking of making?" Dad asked.

"I'll probably make a film tribute to something," I said. I didn't want to let on that the idea included possibly taking over the Wackfords.

"Been a while since your last movie," he said.

"Don't remind me."

James had written up a script for another film, called *J'ai un Loulou Grand Comme le Montana Collé à Mes Fesses*, which translates to "I Have a Booger the Size of Montana Stuck to My Buttocks." The whole thing was going to be in French, which would have instantly made it all kinds of artsy, but it never really got off the ground. I figured that when the time came to make another film, it would have to be something other than avant-garde—we'd already been there and done that, and there was no sense repeating ourselves. Still, it was hard to come up with a way to do something less weird than an avant-garde sex-ed movie without looking like we were going mainstream. The more I thought about it, the more I thought that something that criticized the new downtown might be just the thing we needed. It might be more watchable than something avant-garde, but it could also be controversial. And it might just help Sip stay in business.

When we got home, I stuck *The Wildewood Singers Sing the Beatles* on the wall next to *Saved* by the Voices of Carbondale, which featured even more middle-aged people wearing tacky matching suits and a whole lot of hair spray. I've said it before and I'll say it again: I really don't know what the hell people were thinking in the 1970s. I mean, people in the fifties had a pretty good excuse for any bad album covers they made—they were all living under the notion that they were going to be blown up at any moment, a feeling to which I was no stranger myself. And in the sixties they were reacting to war and other forms of turbulence. But there's just no excuse for the kind of crap they were putting on album covers in the 1970s. Maybe after the Beatles broke up, people found themselves leaderless and adrift.

I spent the rest of the night thinking about Anna and Jenny and all that business. I tried to get my head back into the new movie, or even Sip, but it just didn't work.

Monday morning came around, and I got to school early so I could see Anna before she went inside. I waited by the flagpole until I saw her coming. It's always weird when you finally see someone in the flesh after thinking about practically nothing but that person for a while.

"Hey," she said, smiling. "You do realize it's colder than penguin shit out here, right?"

"Yeah," I said. "Just thought I'd wait for you."

She smiled. And I know this is the kind of thing that makes me seem like I deserve a good punch in the face, but when she smiled, it was like it wasn't cold anymore. All the doubts I'd had, all the thoughts that I might be better off with Jenny, just vanished.

"How was the city?" I asked.

"It was okay," she said. "I had to spend most of the day bumming around the university library while Dad worked. But after that we went and ate at this joint that had live jazz and really good espresso."

"Did you drink it straight?"

"Three shots."

Espresso is sort of an extra-extra-strong form of coffee. It's like concentrating an entire mug of coffee into a little plastic cup from a preschool girl's tea set, and it tastes remarkably bitter. It's not for amateurs. I could only take it if it was mixed into an insane amount of milk, and Anna was drinking it straight. I felt like a total wimp.

Not to mention that a day with *my* dad would have involved bumming around the thrift store while he looked for new ways to blow up the garage, then eating grilled rabbit while he pretended to be a hillbilly, not studying history and listening to jazz. The closest thing to there being any espresso present would be if he and my mother decided to drink shots of ketchup.

As I've said, sometimes with Anna, I felt like I was in over my head.

And now I'd never learn to drink espresso, with Sip going out of business. I had planned on telling Anna about it that morning, but she seemed to be in enough of a good mood that I didn't want to wreck it. It would wreck her day for sure, and I didn't want her to think of me as the guy who had wrecked her day. I know it was paranoid and all that. But still. Seeing Anna helped me stop worrying about Jenny, but it also forced me to think about Sip and Wackfords again.

My first class that day was history with Coach Wilkins, the most hyperactive teacher in Cornersville Trace. He was always jumping up and down, pounding his desk with his fist, and screaming at the top of his lungs. We'd made it as far into American history as World War I, an accomplishment he'd celebrated by doing an impression of a soldier being attacked by mustard gas.

Toward the end of the period, Coach Hunter came into the room.

"Hey, Gene," said Coach Wilkins.

"Ron," said Coach Hunter, nodding. "I found this poem in my office, and I thought it might be by a suicidal student. Wanna give it a look?"

I sank a little bit in my desk as he handed the sheet of paper to Wilkins, who read it to himself.

" 'Locker Room Mausoleum Sutra,' " he said out loud. "This is pretty heavy stuff. But it's about a suicidal gym teacher, not a suicidal student."

Coach Hunter looked right at me. "It was one of you punks, wasn't it?" he asked.

"I don't know what you're talking about," I said.

"I'll just bet you don't," he said.

Everyone in the room turned and looked at me. They were probably sure I was behind whatever the problem was, too.

"Now, hold on, Gene," said Coach Wilkins. "I don't think this is quite Leon's style."

"Yeah, but I'll bet you know who did it, right?" asked Coach Hunter, still staring at me. I felt like I was being interrogated. Maybe he'd drag me back to his office, sit me down in a chair beneath a bare, swinging lightbulb, and beat me senseless until I confessed.

"I don't know anything about it," I said. "Can I read the poem?"

"I'll read it out loud," said Coach Wilkins. "It's pretty good."

And he did, snapping his fingers and trying to do a beatnik voice as he read.

"Locker Room Mausoleum Sutra
By No One in Particular

"The marines didn't want him anymore.
Sent him packing with a cheap vinyl suitcase,
two dollars, forty-seven cents,
and an existential crisis
that got him through three states
on the bus home.
And every locomotive that came rolling by
said, 'There sits a broken man,'
and every siren sounded like a whistle
until he knelt before the school board,
who tapped his shoulder with

an old birch pointer
and said, 'We dub thee Coach.'
Instead of training recruits to go to war,
he trained teenybopper girls to play volleyball
and disinfected locker rooms
until they smelled
pinched and pungent, like the mausoleum
in the veterans' cemetery, where
he knew he'd never rest.
And every yellow school bus
that came rolling by
said, 'There sits a broken man,'
and the whistle sounded like a siren
that he wished would come for him."

"I don't see what the big deal is," I said. "It's just a depressing poem."

"Me neither," said Coach Wilkins. "I don't think there's any rule against putting poems into someone's office, anyway."

"Well, there ought to be," Coach Hunter said. He fixed me with one of those classic "I'll get you for this" looks that gave me the distinct impression that gym class wouldn't be much fun for me that day. Less fun than usual, even.

A few seconds later, Hunter was out the door. I leaned over to where this kid called Jonas was sitting. Jonas was one of those people who try to be funny but are actually just annoying. But I couldn't help talking to him—he always laughed at my jokes.

"Gee," I said, "now, who at this school would possibly want to harm the kindly old gym teacher?"

"Ha ha ha," Jonas laughed. "*Leon.*" That was the way

Jonas laughed. He'd actually say "ha ha ha," then he'd say the name of whoever had told the joke, with so much emphasis that he could be described as saying it in italics. He even laughed at Coach Wilkins. Every five or ten minutes, I'd hear him going "Ha ha ha . . . *Coach Wilkins!*" But I couldn't help trying to crack him up from time to time. It's like, that's what he was there for.

At lunch, I told Dustin and James all about it, and they acted like I'd just told them their army had won the First World War.

"So he not only got it, but he was depressed by it? Croll!" said James.

"Hey," said Dustin, "I don't mess around. If I write a poem to depress someone, you'd better believe they're going to be depressed."

"How did you even get it into the office?" I asked.

"It's almost never locked," said James smugly. "I collect things from it."

"No way," I said, though I honestly wasn't surprised.

"Sure," he said. "It's the sport of Spanish kings!"

"Like what kind of stuff?"

"Little things like whistles," said James. "Not stuff that could really get me busted, like his grade book or his computer. You can really get it for that."

James wasn't really the shoplifting type or anything—I never felt like I should count the change in my pocket after he left—but he sure did pick interesting things to collect. His other hobby was collecting Neighborhood Watch signs.

Toward the end of lunch, I talked about getting *The Wildewood Singers Sing the Beatles* for my wall.

"You know, Leon," James said, "I gotta say it. The bad album covers are fun and all, but your thing last year of covering a wall with speakers was more . . . ambitious, you know?"

"It was more dangerous, too," I said. "The first time I tried them I knocked all the electricity out, and the second time the garage caught fire."

"Yeah," said James. "But it was still cooler."

"Well," I said, "these albums are uncool by definition. That's what makes them cool. Camp value, you know?"

"I'm not saying it isn't," said James, though he still sounded skeptical.

"It's not as bad as my parents' hobby," I said. "This week they've been dressing like hicks and calling each other Lester and Wanda while they cook food out of this nasty cookbook about grilling."

"How's that so much worse?" asked James.

"It is . . . ," I said. "At least I'm being ironic. I'm not sure they are."

"I don't know," said Anna. "The whole grilling thing sounds kind of fun."

I felt a few of my inner organs churning. Like she'd just crammed her hand into my stomach, going in through my belly button, and was jiggling my guts around.

"But it's dorkier than the album covers, right?" I said.

"Well, the album covers are funny," said Anna. "I mean, they're a bit dorky, too, but they're funny."

At that moment, I wished she'd just move up from jiggling my internal organs and squeeze the life out of me altogether. Just find my windpipe, squeeze, and hang on.

I mean, even my dad knew that the album covers

weren't as dorky as the food disasters. Here I was, trying to feel like I could keep up with Anna and her dad, in terms of overall coolness, and she had to go and endorse my parents' embarrassing hobby while calling mine dorky. When I thought about it later, I realized that she hadn't actually been bad-mouthing me, or really even giving my parents a ringing endorsement, but it felt like she was. Combine this with the fact that Sip had six months to live, which I still hadn't gotten around to telling anybody, and I was starting to feel way worse than any of Dustin's poems could ever make a person feel.

As fate would have it, my next class was gym. And as I'd suspected, Coach Hunter made the whole class feel like an interrogation. When we ran laps around the gym, he ran alongside me.

"Who was it, Leon?" he asked. "Which of you put that poem in my office?"

"I don't know!" I sputtered.

"Then you won't mind dropping and giving me twenty, will you?"

Four times over the course of the class, he made me drop and give him twenty. I wished I had been carrying enough cash that I could just drop down and give him a twenty-dollar bill—I would have gladly paid it to get out of the push-ups.

And he kept making it rough on me. All through class, all I heard was "Harris! Let's see those arms!" and "Harris! Get that butt in the air!" It was almost exactly the way my grandfather described the army. But I didn't crack. He couldn't make me talk.

I was practically delirious by the end of the period, feeling half dead, and nearly ready to just give up on trying to be with Anna, if it could make me feel like this. I wanted to just bury myself in the nearest hole and let worms come and suck my eyes out of their sockets. If I were with Jenny, I would be the cool one, not the wannabe. It would be a much easier pace to maintain.

But I wanted Anna.

I know it sounds incredibly geeky, but I wanted her to think I was cool and sophisticated and intellectual. I wanted her to think I was gutsy and dangerous and dark. Maybe the reason we hadn't moved any further than occasional kissing and the whole "are we or aren't we" crap was that she wasn't sure I was ready for that kind of thing. What would happen if she met someone who was? Surely it wouldn't be hard for her to find a guy who knew better than to think there was anything cool about *The Wildewood Singers Sing the Beatles*.

After the school day ended, I waited for Anna outside as I usually did, but I didn't say much to her; we just walked along to the edge of the parking lot and she acted the same as ever, as though she hadn't implied at lunch that I was just as dorky as, if not dorkier than, my parents. I didn't try to kiss her, or make a move like I was going to. When she turned to go, she smiled, and I offered a kind of a weak smile back, and I walked straight home, going in through the front door and up to my room, where I stared up at the bad album covers above my bed.

The Voices of Carbondale. The Wildewood Singers. *Satan Is Real*. I felt like I should tear every one of them down from the wall and take them back to the thrift store from whence they came.

Maybe it was true. Maybe I was just too much of a dork

for Anna. I wasn't dangerous enough. I was going to end up just like my dad—working some dull job, killing time with embarrassing hobbies. I probably wouldn't even have the nerve to get a Mohawk.

I was the biggest dork in school. I looked up at the albums on my wall and tried to do a Jonas-style laugh. "Ha ha ha," I went. "*Satan.*"

Damn. I was good at it.

Dad got home from work shortly thereafter, delighting Mom with stories about how his boss freaked out when he saw the green Mohawk and started saying he was going to fire him. Dad had threatened to quit accounting to become an accounting consultant, and his boss had immediately shut up and let him get back to work.

A short while later, he put on his John Deere cap and started pretending to be Lester, walking around and talking about how he'd "kilt him a barr" for dinner that night, just like either Davy Crockett or Jed Clampett. He wasn't sure which. My mother, in her Wanda outfit, said he'd better not make too much noise while he grilled it.

"I'm sick and tired of hearin' you talk while I'm watchin' my stories!" she said.

"Woman!" said Dad/Lester, "I got a story for you! The story of a True American who kilt him a barr to keep his fam'ly fed!"

While I was being called a dork for my hobbies, this guy had been out scoring points on his boss after showing up with a Mohawk.

If I'd felt so inclined, I probably could have written the poem that would push Coach Hunter over the edge right then and there. But I didn't. Instead, I made up my mind that things were going to be different, and decided to act before I chickened out and changed my mind.

I picked up the phone and called Edie.

"Yeah?" she said. Telephone manners were not her strong suit. It's entirely possible that she was morally opposed to them.

"Hey," I said. "It's Leon. I'm in for your movie idea. The takeover. And not just setting up an office in Wackfords, but taking it over. The pirate thing."

"No way," she said, incredulous. "You and Anna were saying it was all illegal and too risky and stuff."

"Yeah," I said, "but what good is security, anyway? In today's job market, it's not like we'd be throwing away promising futures."

"Security is superstition, and you must live a daring life, or not live at all," said Edie. "Helen Keller said that. Did you know she was a Socialist?"

"Can't say that I did," I said. "But seriously, I think we should take over the Wackfords and turn it into an office, and stop people from buying anything. And make a movie out of it."

"Seriously? You think we can do it?"

"I think we have to," I said. "You know George, the owner of Sip?"

"Vaguely."

"I heard him talking to Troy and Trinity. And he said Sip is going out of business in about six months. Because of the Wackfords, I assume."

"Well, all right, then!" said Edie. "We have to take them

over—maybe we can stop them before Sip closes! Is Anna in, too?"

"I don't know," I said. "I'll have to convince her, I guess."

"No kidding?" asked Edie. "I figured she probably talked you into it."

"Well, she didn't," I said. "You think I'm not enough of a risk taker?"

"Okay, okay," she said. "I believe you."

"I'll talk her into it tomorrow at lunch," I said. "Just leave it to me."

When I hung up, I was already starting to feel good again. Or better, anyway. Maybe getting out of that in-school suspension alive a few months before had made me sort of complacent. Deep down, maybe I'd felt that since I'd already made a bit of a splash with *La Dolce Pubert*, I could just relax for a while. Maybe I *was* getting to be a little bit dorky. Helen Keller was right—you have to do something daring every now and then.

Taking over the Wackfords might not prove any real point. It might not save Sip. But at least I'd be doing something.

I went downstairs, brewed a pot of coffee, and drank it black.

• • • • •

The next morning was the first activity period of the semester. The semester before, I'd had "advanced studies," an activity led by Mr. Streich back before he was in charge of the gifted pool. That was the class I actually did the avant-garde movie for. This semester, they hadn't offered advanced studies

81

as an activity at all, probably just because of my movie. I hated to think I'd ruined it for everyone else.

Since I was sick on the sign-up day, I wasn't able to sign up for the art history activity Anna was taking, or even the politics one Edie would be terrorizing. By the time I got to sign up for an activity, most things were full, and I was left with a choice between Skills for the Job Market and something called Social Problems, which I imagined was full of those stupid things where you read a short story about someone dealing with peer pressure and then discuss how they should react. I didn't want to meet the kids who signed up for either of those very much, and decided on Skills for the Job Market strictly by tossing a coin.

I knew I was in hell even before the bell rang. The class was mostly a bunch of "career track" kids who were already working on their college applications and reading books about how to be a rich asshole instead of just a regular asshole. There were kids there who had joined the football team because it would be "a good place to make connections."

Joe Griffin, the biggest religious creep in school, was there, too. His dad was a sleazy ambulance-chasing lawyer who advertised on television, and he seemed to think he was God's own Angel of Judgment, vested with powers to tell the rest of us we were going to burn in hell. Joe had been instrumental in getting me suspended over *La Dolce Pubert*. He later apologized for that, and I forgave him, but he was still a creep. He sat in the front row of Skills for the Job Market. I couldn't see his face, since I naturally sat in the back, but I imagined that he looked awfully smug, as usual. All the kids there looked pretty smug.

The teacher was a social studies guy called Mr. Morton who always tried to come off as a dynamic young go-getter. He was wearing an orange button-down shirt with a yellow tie, a combination that made him look like he was dressed as a fruit smoothie or something. He spoke fairly rapidly and quite confidently, and talked about what a great leader he was for the first ten minutes. Humility was clearly not a virtue the guy treasured—but the rest of the kids ate it up.

For the first class, his topic was motivation. He recommended putting up those motivational posters, the ones my dad loved so dearly, in our "study environment." Joe Griffin then told him he'd be granted more success if he used posters with Bible verses on them.

"If that's what inspires you, go for it," said Mr. Morton. "You should surround yourself with inspiration." I wondered how many of these jerks would be putting up pictures of Mr. Morton.

"I'm inspired by porn," I said. "Should I fill my study area with centerfolds?"

Joe turned around and gave me a dirty look.

"Stick with the motivational sayings," said Mr. Morton. "Porn would give you the wrong kind of inspiration." Everybody snickered, and Mr. Morton went right back to talking about how great he was.

"I'm not going to be teaching social studies forever," he said. "Just a couple of years. It's the kind of experience a lot of companies love to see. You see, you can't just get a job by having a college degree anymore. You need things to fill out the resume, and working as a teacher in a successful school will make me much more desirable to employers. After a couple of years, I'll use what I've learned here to help me out in the business world."

Well, I thought, I'm very happy to be your guinea pig. I hope I teach you well, dingle-dorf. When the bell rang, I was the first one out the door.

I practically ran down the hall and ended up being the first one to arrive in Coach Wilkins's history class, except for Coach Hunter, who came in at the same time as me.

Coach Wilkins nodded at me and smiled as I took my seat, then turned his attention to Coach Hunter.

"How 'bout it, Gene?" asked Coach Wilkins.

"I found another one," Hunter grumbled. He held out a sheet of paper, and I pricked up my ears.

"Let me see," said Coach Wilkins. It was "The Final Push-up," the one Dustin had read at Sip. Wilkins read it and chuckled. "It's hardly vulgar," he said.

"Whatever," said Coach Hunter. "I'm at the end of my rope, Ron. In this one, it sounds like they want me to put my head in the oven! Hang on to it in case I need it for evidence."

"It's just a poem, Gene," said Wilkins. "It can't hurt anybody."

"That's what you think," he said. He then turned and looked right at me. "Who was it, Harris? If you don't tell me now, there's going to be a locker search of every one of you gifted-pool types."

"That can't be legal," I said. "Do you have a warrant?"

"You don't need a warrant for locker searches, actually," said Coach Wilkins. "The lockers are school property, not student property. But I think he has a point, Gene. What makes you so sure it was someone from the gifted pool?"

84

"Who else is it gonna be?" he asked.

"I'll keep my ears open, Gene," said Coach Wilkins. "But I think your best course of action is to ignore it."

"This is out of hand, Harris," said Coach Hunter. "I'm turning every one of these in to Dr. Brown. If I find out you've been holding out on me, you're in enormous trouble. You and every last one of your friends!"

"I'm not sure that's legal," I said.

"I don't think it is, Gene," said Coach Wilkins. "You might have a case if the poems were threatening or obscene, but there's no rule against poems that are just depressing. If Leon hears anything, I'm sure he'll let you know."

And he winked at me as Coach Hunter left. I hate it when teachers wink at me. And I'm pretty sure they only wink at kids they think are dorky enough to think it's cool. All the more reason to become a pirate, I figured.

When the class filled up, Coach Wilkins went into his usual routine, and Jonas spent the whole class period using his fingernail to scrape at a crayon. About midway through the class, he tapped me on the shoulder to get my attention and showed me that he'd been sculpting it to look like a penis.

"Cram it, Jonas," I muttered, rolling my eyes.

"Ha ha ha," said Jonas, thinking I was being funny. *"Leon."*

Two hours later, at lunch, I relayed Coach Hunter's latest rant to James and Dustin, who were thrilled.

"Man," Dustin said. "Two days' worth of my poems and the guy's already out of energy. I'm a king, man!"

"Yeah," I said. "And I get to be your whipping boy. You should see what he's doing to me in gym!"

Anna came in and nudged me in the arm.

"Hey," I said. "I've got something to tell you."

"Go for it."

"I think we should go ahead with the pirate thing."

She took a sip of Coke and then looked at me with an eyebrow raised. She had the cutest eyebrows I could possibly imagine, and when she raised one of them, that alone could usually get me to change my mind about something. But I was resolved to stand firm.

"Edie's idea?" she asked. "The illegal one? I thought we were just going to set up an office there."

"We could only do that for a few minutes before someone kicked us out," I said. "We need something more drastic. It looks like Sip is going to be closing this summer."

"No way!" she said. "How do you know?"

"I heard George talking to Troy about it."

"No shit? I should have known. Those bastards!"

"So we've got to take Wackfords over. Instead of just pretending that there's an office in there, we'll actually take it over like pirates and try to stop people from buying coffee. Make a stand. I'm even game for getting arrested right about now."

She paused for a second and played with the little metal thingie on top of her Coke can. "It's still kind of a risk, though," she said. "Even if it's a nonviolent takeover. They might try to make an example out of us."

"Sure, it's a risk," I said. "That's part of what makes it such a good idea for a movie. And I'm into risk taking."

"I still don't know," she said. And she pulled a sandwich out of her bag and started eating. A second later Brian and Edie showed up at the table.

"Man, you wouldn't believe the kids in the politics activity," said Edie, clearly annoyed. "I don't think they've ever met a communist before."

"Well, isn't that obvious?" I asked.

She rolled her eyes. "It's like I'm a monkey on display for them in there," she said. "But I'm the only one who knows anything about politics." She smiled, obviously quite pleased with herself. "Anyway, Leon, did you talk Anna into it?"

"Not yet he didn't," said Anna cheerfully. "I keep thinking we can find a better way to do it that won't get us arrested."

"If we get arrested, we'll be legends," said Edie. "And it's a small price to pay if it might save Sip."

"I don't know if we can save Sip like this," I said. "It's probably too late for that. George has probably signed all the papers and stuff. But we can at least make a blow for them before they go."

"Yeah," said Anna, "but is striking a blow worth going to prison?"

"Small price to pay," said Edie. "We're all under eighteen, so we wouldn't be locked up for long. Then when we get out, we can get jobs on the lecture circuit or something."

I laughed. "Oh, God," I said. "I'd be a motivational speaker."

Now Anna was smiling for the first time since I'd told her Sip was closing. "You? A motivational speaker?" she asked.

"Sure," I said, "why not?" Somehow, her thinking the idea of my being a motivational speaker was funny bothered me a lot less than her thinking my records were kind of dorky. I deepened my voice and said, "Make yourself invaluable and there's no limit to what you can do!"

"Yes," she said, deepening her own voice, like she was doing a really bad impression of me, "you, too, can succeed in life by going to jail before you're even in high school. Believe in yourself and anything is possible!"

Anna moved over ever so slightly and put her hand on my knee. I just about melted.

By the end of lunch, we hadn't really reached any conclusions about what to do about taking over the Wackfords, and Anna hadn't done anything to indicate that she thought I *wasn't* a bit of a dork, but I felt immeasurably better. About everything. Even if she did think I was a dork, I felt like she was okay with that. Maybe she even *liked* it. And even if Sip was closing, we'd at least be able to help make sure it went out with a bang, leaving a documentary about how much better than the Wackfords it was.

Gym class was a repeat of the day before, but I was in a much better mood. I ran the laps and just ignored it when Coach Hunter shouted things about where my butt ought to be. In fact, when he told me to get it up in the air, I wiggled it around a bit and got a laugh from the kids who noticed.

After I finished cruising through the rest of the day, I met up with Anna outside school, just like normal.

"I think I figured it out," she said. "I know how we can make the takeover work."

"Really?" I asked. "How?"

"Mutiny," she said. "We're going to turn Troy into a pirate."

6

Turning Troy into a pirate didn't seem like it would be impossible—he didn't seem to be dripping with company loyalty or anything. He'd even offered to help us find a good time to set up an office. I spent most of the rest of the day coming up with more ideas as to how to make the movie work and trying to decide exactly what kind of point we could make by taking over the Wackfords.

Just on the off chance that I'd started to think my troubles were over and things weren't going to be complicated or weird from here on out, about an hour after I got home, I got a phone call from Anna.

"Can you call Jenny?" she asked. "I tried to get her to join us for the movie, but she's nervous. Maybe you'll have better luck."

I sat still for a second. Did she know that Jenny liked me? If she did, would she be bringing this up at all? Most people wouldn't, but then again, Anna wasn't most people.

"I can try, I guess," I said.

"Good," Anna said. "So you call her up. I'll work on arranging another summit meeting. Just the pirates."

"Okay," I said. "You want to meet tomorrow?"

"Tonight," said Anna. "Sip at eight. We'll plot for tomorrow then."

"Okay."

We hung up, and I stared at the phone, trying to get my nerve up, for quite a while.

But reasoning that it was Anna's idea, not mine, I finally dialed Jenny's number, then said all the right things about schoolwork to get past her parents.

"Leon!" Jenny said as she took the phone. "More homework questions?"

"Yeah," I said, "I was wondering if you understood the bifactoring of the square root of the prime directive on the third . . ."

"It's okay," she said. "I'm out of their earshot. We can talk like normal people."

"Hmm," I said. "I'm not really sure I know how to do that."

She laughed. "You're so funny, Leon. What's up?"

"Well," I said, "I heard you were worried about helping us with the movie, and I thought I'd call and try to convince you."

"God, Leon," she said. "You just, like, make me melt."

Okay. I blushed and shook my head a little bit. I was just trying to tell her about a movie project, not come on to her. I had to sort of admire her frankness, though. I couldn't have brought myself to say something like that to someone I liked for anything. Not even Anna, even though she knew it.

"Well, anyway," I said, ignoring her comment, "we want

you to join in on it. We're meeting at Sip at eight." If it sounds like I wasn't really trying to convince her, it's because I wasn't. Having to work with both her and Anna would be all kinds of awkward.

"Oh my God, that would be so cool . . . but there's no way. Just sneaking out to Sip is hard for me; if I snuck to Wackfords and took it over and my parents found out, they'd probably send me to reform school."

"That's totally understandable," I said, feeling greatly relieved.

"But anyway," she said, "thanks for thinking about me, okay?"

"Sure," I said. "See you in school."

Well. That could have gone worse, I suppose. I still wasn't sure where she got off thinking it was okay to tell me I made her melt, considering she knew all about me and Anna and everything. But on the other hand . . . I sort of had to admit I liked it. Who wouldn't want a girl to say he made her melt? I imagine that even a gay guy would be pretty flattered.

An hour later, I went downstairs, knowing that I was going to need a ride to Sip at eight, and found my dad in the garage, mixing a bunch of green gunk together in a beaker.

"Hi, Leon," he said. "Watch this!"

He put down the beaker, which looked like it had formerly been a mayonnaise jar. It was full of some stuff that I really hoped was not bear snot but that looked like it couldn't be much else. I suppose it could have been some other kind of snot, except that there was too much of it for it to have come out of a human.

"What is that?" I asked.

"It's a lot of things," he said. "And it's about halfway to being a new prototype for the hair dye. And check out what happens when I heat it way up!"

He lit a Bunsen burner, then picked up the jar of bear snot (or whatever it was) with some tongs and held it over the flame. Nothing happened for a few seconds, but slowly, the color started to change. The inside of it started to look like it was almost glowing or something, and gradually, the glow spread until the whole pile of snot was glowing green.

"Whoa!" I said. "That's awesome!" Finally, a practical use for chemistry besides blowing things up: making stuff glow.

He took the jar off the flame and the stuff stopped glowing and went back to looking like regular snot. "Pretty cool, huh?" he said.

"And that stuff is supposed to dye hair but not skin?"

"Well, not yet, but it's getting there. I'll be ready for an actual test tomorrow night. Care to volunteer?"

"I'll pass, actually," I said. "When you know you have a working model, we'll talk, but I won't be the lab rat."

"Fair enough."

I hadn't really considered getting green hair myself; I sort of worried that if I did, I'd just look like I was trying to keep up with my dad. On the other hand, though, it might be fun to tell people my dad had given me green hair. Maybe I could say it was a form of creative punishment my parents had read about in some parenting magazine.

"Anyway," I said, "can I get another ride to Sip after dinner tonight, like, at eight?"

"I don't see why not," he said. "Maybe I'll come in my-self for once. I wouldn't mind a good cup of coffee."

"Um . . . okay," I said, trying not to let on that I was ter-rified. It would be awfully hard for anyone to plot a takeover with their father sitting at the table—unless he thought it was a good idea and wanted to help, which was a distinct possibility. But that could be even worse.

Dinner, to my great relief, was not a food disaster that night—just regular tuna casserole. It wasn't tuna with Spam casserole, or tuna and liver pâté, or watermelon tuna, just regular tuna casserole, and my parents called each other by their actual names, not Lester and Wanda. The Grilled American food wasn't really that bad, as far as the food disasters went, but I couldn't handle another dinner with Lester and Wanda right then.

Ten minutes after the table was cleared, Dad put on his knit cap, and we drove off toward Sip.

"So," he said, "what's good at this place?"

"Oh, it's all pretty good," I said. "I usually just get the cof-fee, personally. Sometimes I have a mocha or something."

"I like a good cup of coffee," he said. "But I can't get used to it being expensive. I remember when coffee was a dime."

"Oh yeah, those were the days," I said, trying to sound like an old man. "Back in my day coffee hadn't even been invented yet. We just poured some mud into hot water. And in those days, most of my friends had named like Ugh and Grunt."

"Oh really?" said my dad, appropriately amused.

"And we didn't have coffee shops, just caves with better-than-average mud. And we didn't have cars to drive to those, oh no. We had wagon trains. And these caves didn't serve sandwiches—we had to eat poor Ugh. But he was an accountant, so no one was too sorry."

"Okay," Dad said, even though he was chuckling a bit. "I'm not that old. Your mom and I haven't even started to talk about moving to Florida yet."

"I know, I know," I said. "But I wouldn't recommend complaining about the cost of coffee in there."

"Of course not," he said. "It's a coffee shop. You expect people to be snotty in those places. I'm not that clueless, you know."

"And don't get too attached to it," I said. "I overheard the owner say they're closing in six months."

"Figures," he grumbled.

All the while, as we drove along, I was plotting a way I could ditch Dad once we got inside. I was pondering it all down Venture Street.

As it turned out, though, I didn't have to worry. Inside Sip, I saw Anna, Brian, and Edie all sitting in our usual corner, and in an opposite corner, Anna's dad was sitting and chatting with Trinity.

"Warren!" said my dad.

Anna's dad smiled. "Hi, Nick," he said. "Grab a chair!"

My dad walked over to the table and took a seat.

"Hey," Trinity greeted him.

"Nice blue hair!" said my dad. "Check mine out!"

And he whipped off his knit cap to show her the green Mohawk. She sort of looked like a deer caught in headlights for a second, then started laughing.

"Do you believe it, Warren?" my dad said. "I'm hip!"

"It's adorable!" said Trinity, running her fingers through it.

Compared to Warren Brandenburg, my dad was probably the least hip person in all of suburbia—and that's saying something. I slinked away from him, using my good old ninja swiftness, and gravitated toward the table where Brian, Edie, and Anna were sitting. There was no sign of Jenny.

"Your dad came too, huh?" Anna asked. "Mine insisted." She rolled her eyes a bit.

"I don't mind if he wants a cup of coffee now and then," I said. "I just don't see why he had to pick the day we're planning a piracy."

"Anyway," she said, "since they're both here, we may only have a minute, so let's get started. We've gathered here tonight, at the last independent coffee shop in Cornersville Trace, to become pirates."

"Avast!" said Brian. Edie patted him on the head.

"Though our original plan was merely to make a movie contrasting the old downtown with the new, including a scene of us setting up an office in Wackfords to see if anyone even noticed," Anna went on, "recent events necessitate more action. So the mission is as follows: as soon as we can determine that it's feasible, we'll arrange to take over the Wackfords on Cedar Avenue. We'll decorate it to look like an accounting and midlevel management strategies office and attempt to disrupt coffee sales, inviting people who want a proper cup of coffee to go to Sip."

"Should we talk a bit about what sort of point we're supposed to be proving?" I asked.

"The point of the takeover is to get people to go to Sip," Anna said. "And the point of the movie will be to show that the old downtown is cooler than the new one. Sip is a place where you go for intellectual discussions and stuff like that, whereas Wackfords is a place where you go to set up an accounting office."

Brain thought this over. "Sounds reasonable enough," he said. "Plus, it'll be fun."

"Sounds good to me," said Edie. I nodded in agreement.

"All right," said Anna. She dug in her bag and pulled out a yellowy brown sheet of paper and a permanent marker. "Let's put down a charter and mission statement for the crew."

"Mission statement?" said Edie. "That's a bunch of crap."

"All lame offices have mission statements," said Anna, writing "HMS PIRATE SHIP" at the top of the paper. "And I'll bet you anything that Wackfords has one. So if we're starting our own office, we'll need one, too."

"What the hell's a mission statement?" Brian asked.

"It's a bunch of nonsense that businesses throw together to tell what kind of business they intend to do," I said. "Most of the time, it's just a bunch of buzzwords and gobbledygook."

"Well," said Edie, "maybe ours can be that mission statements suck!"

"Yes!" I said. "That should be our mission statement. 'Mission statements suck.' "

Anna shrugged. "All righty," she said. And she wrote it down in capital letters.

"We don't need to sign in blood or anything, right?"

"We should!" said Edie, reaching for one of the safety pins on her coat.

Anna, to my great relief, shook her head as she folded up the charter. "That wouldn't be very sanitary," she said.

We will probably go down in history as the first pirates ever to be all that concerned with sanitation.

"All right," said Brian. "So we have a crew, and we have a mission."

"And I have a camera we can use," I said.

"Me too," said Brian.

"All right," said Edie. "What do we do next?"

"Next up is the mutiny," said Anna. "If we're gonna pull off a takeover, we'll need inside help. We'll need to get Troy to join the crew."

"Or at least work with us," I said.

Edie grinned. "I love it!" she said. "Treachery on the high seas of Cedar Avenue!"

"He will join us or die," said Brian, a bit over-dramatically.

"So it's all set, then," said Anna. "Tomorrow, after school, we'll meet at the flagpole and set sail for Wackfords to organize a mutiny."

"I don't know," said Edie. "I signed a petition online saying I'd never go there."

"It doesn't count if you're going there to plot to over-throw it," said Anna. "And you'll have to go there sooner or later for the takeover. We'll need to go and recruit Troy to start with, and we'll need to get a good feel for the whole layout of the place and make a map."

"Arrr!" said Brian. "An 'X' will mark the spot!"

"So tomorrow while we're there, everyone try to memorize the layout so we can draw up a map of the inside of the store. So we're all agreed to set sail tomorrow?"

"Agreed," said Edie.

Anna put her hand out in the middle of the table, and Edie put her hand on top of it. Brian and I put our hands on top of that.

"Then I declare the crew of the HMS Pirate Ship to be officially formed," Anna said. And we all withdrew our hands.

"What do you mean about this HMS Pirate Ship business?" said Brian. "We don't really have a ship."

Anna shrugged. "It's just a gimmick," she said. "It's also a redundancy. Her Majesty's ship Pirate Ship."

All of a sudden, the music changed from tango to a fast punk song.

"Yes!" Edie said. "Johnny Christmas and the Kindergarteners!"

I looked over at the other corner. Trinity was walking back over to my dad and Warren's table, where my dad was bouncing around in his seat.

"This is great!" he shouted. "Who's singing?"

"This is Johnny Christmas!" said Trinity as she started to move to the music herself.

"Totally tubular!" said my dad.

"Oh, God," I said as I sank as low as I could in my chair.

"Do punks say 'totally tubular'?" asked Brian.

Edie shook her head, but she was obviously trying not to laugh.

"Seeing as how we're pirates," I said quietly, "did anyone

happen to bring a dagger? Because it would really help me out if someone would stab me to death right now."

Trinity was really dancing now; I was impressed by her graceful, conservative pogoing. To my great horror, my dad jumped up to join her, and soon they were both jumping up and down, though only Trinity seemed to have a handle on the concept that you're supposed to jump up and down to the beat of the music. My dad was just jumping randomly. I'm not much of a dancer myself, but I didn't know you could *be* bad at the pogo.

"Rock 'n' roll!" Dad shouted, in a very bad British accent. I prayed that my dad wouldn't realize the song was called "Crotchgrabber Junction," since that would probably inspire him to, well, grab his crotch.

"Since when does your dad have a Mohawk?" asked Edie.

"He's working on a new kind of hair dye that only sticks to hair, not to skin or anything," I said. "And he tested it on himself."

"Sweet!" said Edie. "After I did the red streaks in my hair, I never got the stains out of my towel. It looked like I'd cleaned up after someone got shot or something."

"Well," said Brian, "isn't that what punk rock is all about?"

The song sped up a bit. "Leon," Anna whispered in my ear. "You might want to get him out of here before they start slam dancing."

That hadn't occurred to me. I jumped up from the table and practically ran over to them.

"Well, this was fun," I said, grabbing Dad's arm, "but we really must be going."

"But I haven't had my coffee yet!" said Dad.

"We can do that another time," I said, dragging him toward the door. "We need to go home now. You need to get to work on your invention."

"Bye!" Dad shouted as I pulled him outside. He settled down as soon as the cold air hit him. "Man!" he said. "That was fun."

"It was dangerous!" I said.

"Oh, come on," he said. "It was just jumping up and down."

"I know," I said. "But it's a gateway dance. The pogo tends to lead to slam dancing, and then you could have really gotten hurt. Those safety pins in Trinity's dress could have come loose and poked your eye out!"

"Aw," said my dad. "I can take care of myself."

"It's just because we love you, Dad," I said. "Mom and I don't want you to get hurt."

He rolled his eyes. "Whatever," he said.

And we got into the car and drove back home. By the time we were off Cedar Avenue, I was more determined than ever to take over the Wackfords. There is no greater tragedy than when a child has to lecture his parents about safety. Just a few days before, having him pogo dance while I sat there listening to Edie talk about what a good idea one of his inventions was would have ruined my entire week.

But things were different now. I was a pirate.

Fifteen minutes into the school day the next morning, I decided that I never, ever wanted to hear the term "leadership skills" again. It seemed to be by far the most popular topic of conversation among the Skills for the Job Market kids, who were really getting into a discussion about using leadership skills in fast-food and retail work.

Up at the front of the room, Mr. Morton, who was still dressed as a fruit smoothie, but maybe as a different flavor this time, was going on and on about how to present yourself when applying to work as a customer service representative. From what I gathered, he thought you should show up acting like a slick-talking game show host.

"You see," he said, "that's what they look for when they hire new team members. They don't just want team players, they want leaders."

Yeah, I thought. Leaders who will work for just over minimum wage and can lead the other employees into battle against the store across the street. Call me a snot-nosed commie whiner or whatever, but when I think of leaders, I think of guys like Winston Churchill or George Washington, not the assistant housewares manager down at the Mega Mart.

Wackfords, I imagined, was probably big on talking about leadership skills. It seemed like their sort of thing. I wondered what they called their employees. No one actually says "employee" anymore—they all say something like "associate," "teammate," or something equally dumb. If this was the job market, I thought maybe I'd just become a taxi driver. That guy who'd driven our taxi Saturday night probably didn't have an ounce of leadership skills in his entire body, and he did all right.

At the end of the day, Anna, Brian, Edie, and I gathered quietly around the flagpole outside the building. The weather service in the morning had said that it was going to be the coldest day of the year so far, and it certainly felt like it. We'd been able to see our breath hanging in the air for weeks, of course, but this time it felt like it might actually turn into a solid chunk of ice instead of floating away.

"Perfect," said Brian. "We'll have the element of surprise. They'll never expect to be raided by pirates in this weather!"

"Yeah," I said. "Whereas in the summer, it's something they try to stay on the lookout for."

"Why do you think they're always hiring?" Anna asked. "They need people to stand on the roof with spyglasses."

I was wearing my usual jeans and winter coat. Anna was wearing her furry hooded coat, the one that made her look like an Eskimo. Edie was in what I guess was supposed to be a punk ensemble, though it really looked more goth—a rather garish long black coat that blended well with the nonred parts of her hair. Brian was wearing a studded leather jacket that was nowhere near warm enough for the winter over his T-shirt. He didn't even have a hat or a hood or anything—his only headgear was an eye patch.

"Take that thing off," said Edie when she saw it. "You look like a total tool."

"Hell no," said Brian. "If we're gonna be pirates, then I'm going all the way."

"Why not cut off your leg at the knee and get a peg leg, then?" Edie asked.

"Because the school would expel me if they caught me walking around with a saw, but you can make an eye patch from the things you find around the art room. It's easy if you know how."

So we wandered our way up Seventy-sixth Street, past Flowers' Grove Park and the pond, with Anna looking like an Eskimo, Edie looking like a vampire, and Brian looking like a dumbass. We would have made a good cast for one of those movies where a band of misfits go on an incredible journey, which, funnily enough, was pretty much the case.

About midway through the walk, Edie said, "You think we're far enough away?"

"What do you mean?" I asked.

"To be sure we're not being followed?"

There were some cars rumbling along down Seventy-sixth, but there was certainly nobody on the sidewalk. The only people we could see were a couple of kids skating on the frozen pond.

"I think we're pretty safe," I said.

"Obviously," said Anna. "Who'd follow us? It's not fit for man or beast out here."

"The government," Edie said matter-of-factly.

"Arrr!" Brian shouted at the kids on the pond. No one turned to look.

It was about a ten-minute walk up to Cedar Avenue, then a few blocks east to Wackfords. We stood around outside the door for a while, sort of staring at it, not wanting to admit we were nervous.

"Wackfords!" Brian shouted, socking me in the arm.

"Well," said Edie finally. "Here we are."

"Yep," said Brian. "This must be the place."

"Oh, you big babies," said Anna. "Come on!"

And she stomped up to the front door. We all ran after her, not wanting to look like complete wimps. After all, it was cold as hell. No point in standing around in the wind.

Brian jumped in front of Anna and ran inside, shouting, "Yo ho ho, and avast, ye swabs!"

No one really seemed to notice; the place was practically empty. Troy was standing behind a cash register in his green apron; another guy, somewhat older and heavier than Troy, with a bushy black beard, was behind the espresso machine; and a plump blond woman was standing at the counter.

"Hey, guys," said Troy.

"Hey yourself, ye scurvy scalawag!" shouted Brian. Edie ran over to him to try to shut him up. I guessed there was probably something in *The Communist Manifesto* that forbade her to have fun in a Wackfords.

"Is it International Talk Like a Pirate Day already?" asked Troy.

"Nope," said the guy behind the espresso machine. "That's in September."

"What're you guys doing here?" asked Troy. "I thought you guys wouldn't come here on a bet."

"We're plunderin' booty!" said Brian.

"Just came in to say hello," said Anna.

The guy behind the counter put a cup on the counter. "Mezzo caramel freezero," he said. The plump blond woman picked it up.

"Awfully cold for a freezero," said Troy.

"I have a good heater in my car," she said, sounding rather annoyed.

"They don't come warm enough for days like today," said the other guy behind the counter. "I should know. I've been here for thirty-seven years!"

"Yeah," the lady said sarcastically. "You're what, twenty?"

"You know something?" said the guy. "You remind me of my oldest daughter."

The woman shook her head and walked out with her drink.

"Guys," said Troy, "this is Andy Bellow. He's my shift supervisor. That means he's in charge of looking the other way when I break the rules."

"Pleasure's all mine," said Andy, nodding as he slung a whipped-cream dispenser around like a pistol.

"Anyway, Troy," I said. "We have a little proposition for you."

"Go for it."

"Well, as you can see from my dumbass friend's costume, we've decided to become pirates. It's for a pool project."

"You're taking us over, then?" asked Troy. "I thought you just wanted to set up an office in here and see if anyone noticed."

"What's all this?" asked Andy. "We're being taken over?"

"Yes," said Anna. "We're planning to make a movie about taking over a Wackfords and turning it into an office."

"Are we talking guns and stuff?" asked Andy. "I don't mind you setting up an office, but no job is worth getting shot over."

"Of course not," I said. "We'll just come in and set up an office, but we're going to try to stop people from buying coffee."

"What kind of office are we talking about?" Andy was intrigued enough to put the whipped-cream thing on the counter.

"Accounting and midlevel management strategies," said Anna, who sounded as though she'd done this sort of negotiating dozens of times before.

A slow grin spread across Troy's face.

"No kidding," Andy said. "I can't imagine it would be that different from the way they expect me to run this joint any other day."

"That's exactly the point," said Anna. "We'd take over the store for a while, turn it into an accounting office, and see how many people notice the difference. Maybe make some people go to Sip instead. And make a movie out of it."

"Huh," said Andy. "What are you guys, like, a bunch of junior high revolutionaries or something?"

"Just Edie," said Anna. "The rest of us are filmmakers and devotees of the old downtown."

"Well," said Troy, "technically, it's in the handbook that we're not supposed to let anyone film anything inside the store."

"Bunch of corporate crap," said Edie, scowling as she looked around the room. She looked like a Baptist who had just wandered into a Satanic ritual. "That means they have something to hide."

"My thoughts exactly," said Troy. "They don't want anybody to know about the four-year-olds grinding sugar in the back."

"Hey, if these guys take us over, it's no skin off my back," said Andy. "And that thing about filming is buried in the back of the manual. You can plead ignorance. As for me, I was getting ready to move on. When you've mastered whipped-cream-dispenser juggling, it's time to be checking on down the line."

"This is what I was telling you guys about," said Troy. "He's a McHobo."

"It's a way of life," said Andy, looking away from us and out the window. "I've worked at half the places on Cedar. I've been here for six months, and now it's time to move on."

"You never work anywhere longer than six months?" Brian asked.

"Never. That's part of the McHobo code. If you stay

longer than that, you can end up specializing, and to special-ize is to settle. Settling in a retail job is the kiss of death to a McHobo."

"How many places have you worked?" I asked.

"Eighteen," Andy said proudly. "Started getting jobs six years ago, and since then I've been at Grocery World, Grocery Circus, Burger Box, Burger Baron, all the major pizza places. Couple of shoe stores. Another Wackfords. The vitamin store. I worked at Mega Mart for about three hours once, but now I'm not even allowed back in there."

"You should see this guy's bedroom wall," said Troy. "It's lined with all his name tags from his other jobs."

"They're my trophies," said Andy. "Some wannabe McHobos just buy old name tags online, but all of mine are authentic."

"Show them your tattoo, man," said Troy.

Andy put down the whipped-cream dispenser and proudly rolled up his sleeve to show us his shoulder, where there was a tattoo of a name tag with his name on it. Where the store logo would normally have been was the word "wherever." Below the name were the words "McHobos Do It All Over Town!"

"Anyway," said Andy, rolling his sleeve back down, "how can we be of service to this crew of pirates?"

"Actually," said Anna, "we were hoping we could inter-est you in a mutiny."

"Mutiny?" asked Troy. "Keep talking. I got two hours less than I need to qualify for benefits again this week. I'm about ready to start a mutiny of my own."

"Not my fault, man," said Andy. "Harold calls those shots."

"I'm not saying it is," said Troy. "If the world being round was a problem, I'd happily blame it on Harold."

"You should go union!" Edie said with a smirk.

Andy smiled at her. "It's not that easy," he said. "Many are the McHobos who've gone from store to store trying to form unions and failing. But I like the way you pirates think."

"What we're looking for," said Anna, "is someone like you who can help us take control of the store for a while someday soon, and wouldn't mind us breaking some rules."

Andy picked up a white rag and started polishing the whipped-cream dispenser. "Hmm," he said. "Harold wouldn't think much of it."

"So?" asked Troy. He looked over at us. "Harold is the manager. He's very by-the-book about things around here."

"Yes. That's why Harold not thinking much of it makes it all the more attractive," said Andy. "The first time I signed on for a hitch at a Wackfords, over at the Shaker Heights store five years ago, it seemed like they wanted coffee freaks who *wouldn't* go by the book. Now they just want people who yammer on and on about leadership skills."

Aha!

"Well," I said, "why not show some leadership skills and join the rebellion?"

"I knew when the wind changed that something like this was coming," said Andy. "The time has come. Troy and I'll be the only ones here from about five-fifteen till noon on

Saturday. Why don't you guys come by when we open? We won't stop you. It's time for me to get fired."

"You sure you want to get fired?" Anna asked.

"McHobos look for signs to tell us it's time to move on," he explained. "It's been time for a while now—moving up to being a shift supervisor is actually a violation of the McHobo code. So you guys coming in here is a sign, or I don't know what is. But I don't want to just quit this place. I want to go out with a bang. I'll even bring you some desks to use in the office."

Troy nodded at Andy almost reverently.

"If you say so," I said, though I wasn't entirely sure I wanted someone's unemployment hanging over my head.

"Just come by on Saturday. We start up at five-fifteen."

"Do you mean five-fifteen in the morning?" asked Edie.

"Yeah," said Troy. "That's when we get here to start setting up. Store opens at six."

"We'll need time to set up anyway," said Anna. "Five-fifteen'll be fine."

"Just one thing to keep you guys out of trouble," said Andy. "If Harold comes in, you have to tell him you're setting up to sell Girl Scout cookies or something."

"He'll still kick them out," said Troy. "You probably can't do that, either."

"Yeah," said Andy, "but you don't go to jail for selling Girl Scout cookies. I'll take the rap for letting you set up. Good a way as any if I want to get fired."

"Should we be in uniform for that?" asked Brian. "We were going to go for business gear."

I tried to think of Brian in a Girl Scout uniform. If the

cops saw him dressed like that, they'd surely think they'd found a pedophile in Cornersville Trace at last.

"Nah, that won't be necessary," said Andy. "People sell Girl Scout cookies in civilian garb out in the parking lot all the time; I'll tell him we let you inside because it's so cold. Just be here early enough and I'll cover the rest."

"No problem," I said. "Five o'clock it is. We can handle being kicked out eventually, as long as he doesn't arrest us or anything."

"You guys still wanna plunder some booty?" asked Troy. "Here. I'll mark this out as damaged." He picked up a brownish yellow bag of coffee beans and tossed it at Anna, who caught it.

"Wackfords House Blend?" she said, looking down at it. "Good sir, you insult me."

"I didn't say you had to drink it," said Troy. "Maybe you can throw it through somebody's window or something."

Brian snatched it out of Anna's hand. "Avast!" he shouted. "We be plundering this here booty for the crew of the HMS Pirate Ship!"

Behind the counter, Andy snickered. "Yo ho ho and a bottle of organic kiwi juice," he said.

"Tell you what," said Troy. "Come to Sip Friday night at nine, we'll go over all the last-minute details."

"Deal," I said.

"And you have to promise to blur out our faces in the video," said Andy. "It's another rule of the McHobos—never get anyone else in trouble. I don't want Troy to get fired, too."

"I can get fired!" said Troy. "I can go get another name tag job someplace else, too."

"Patience," said Andy. "You're not ready yet."

Troy nodded reverently again.

So we all shook hands and the four of us wandered back outside into the cold wind.

"Holy shit," I said. "We did it. We just organized a mutiny at Wackfords."

"That was way easier than I thought," said Anna. And she grabbed my arm and pulled me in close. I pulled her in closer. It's hard to cuddle through about four layers of clothes, including thick winter coats, but suddenly she was hugging me so tight it felt practically like we were going to second base. She whispered into my ear, "I'd kiss you, but I'm afraid my tongue would get stuck."

"Fair enough," I whispered back.

Clearly, my plan to show I was on her level, not some dork following along behind her, was working.

Brian opened up the bag of coffee beans Troy had given him as plunder and threw it high in the air over a mostly empty strip mall parking lot. The beans came flying out as it fell to the ground, raining down onto the icy blacktop, which made a really cool noise.

"Yo ho ho!" Brian shouted. And you could hear it echo all the way down the street.

Of all the times not to have a camera running.

● ● ● ● ●

By the time I made it home, I was in a great deal of pain. I felt like I could've pulled my face right off of my skull—I imagine it would be a lot like peeling a Fruit Roll-Up off the cellophane—if I could've moved my fingers.

"Leon!" my mother shouted. "You're late! Where've you been?"

"Stayed late at school," I said. "I had to work on a project for my job market skills class."

"You could have called," she said.

"Not really," I said. "They won't let me use my phone at school, and with all my gloves on and stuff, I couldn't have dialed once I got outside."

Sometimes rules backfire on parents; they'd pushed for all the rules against having phones in class back in the days when the only kids who had them were drug dealers. Now everyone had them, and needed to use them to call home, since there weren't any pay phones left, but the parents were stuck with the rules they'd made.

She walked to the door, where I was busy trying to get all my winter gear off and hung up.

"Well," she said, "I guess as long as it was for school, it's okay. I can't blame you for not wanting to take your gloves off in this weather."

I finished getting unbundled and wandered into the kitchen. "You don't happen to have any coffee brewed or anything, do you?" I asked. "Something hot?"

"I'll brew some," she said. "Your dad is in the lab, working on his dye. He'll probably want something hot when he comes in, too."

"Maybe he could focus on inventing a lower-cost heating system," I said.

"Well," she said, "it's not like I haven't tried to get him to invent something that practical over the years. But it's no use—he invents what he feels like inventing."

"Yeah," I said. "And trying to come up with heating systems would probably put him in way more danger than working on dyes, anyway."

It was exactly one second later that we heard a blood-curdling scream coming from the garage. Dad came running into the kitchen, where he quickly stuck his head into the sink.

"*Aaaahhhh!*" he screamed, turning on the water. "Just shoot me! Shoot me! Shoot me!"

"Nick!" said my mother, running over to him. "What happened?"

He growled and groaned while the cold water ran onto his head. "The dye!" he said. "It burns!"

A minute or so later, he'd stopped screaming and turned off the water. He just stood there with his head in the sink, breathing heavily.

"Well," he said, between pants, "I don't think it stuck to my scalp, at least. Rolled right off, just like it was supposed to."

A few seconds later he pulled his head out of the sink and toweled off with a dishrag.

Most of the Mohawk was gone. All that remained was a little patch near the front of his head.

"Yeah," I said, "but I don't think it agreed with your hair."

He paused for a second, then brought his hand ever so slowly up to his head, feeling around where the rest of his Mohawk used to be.

"Oh my God!" he said. "I'm bald!" He then found the remaining patch and heaved a sigh of relief that there was some left.

"I guess it must have burned it off," he said, like a regular crusader for the obvious. He walked into the nearby bathroom to get a look in the mirror. When he saw himself, he made a face like he'd just seen the ghost of somebody really unpleasant. "I made it so it would react to hair but not skin, and I guess it worked. At least my scalp isn't all bloody and blistered, right?"

"Right," I said.

"Well then, I guess it sort of worked," he said. "It just rolled off my skin without leaving a stain. But it sure as hell felt like it was burning!"

Right about then, he stepped out of the bathroom, and my mother started to chuckle. "Well," she said, "I hope you didn't mess up your scalp so much that your hair won't grow back," she said. "You look pretty silly."

"Yeah," I said. "But you looked pretty silly to start with. Now you have a punk Charlie Brown thing going on."

My dad came and sat down at the kitchen table, wrapping the towel around his head. "I thought the Mohawk was cool," he said.

"It would have been," I said, "on somebody else."

"That'll do, Leon," he said. "That'll do."

And he sat staring across the kitchen, through the living room to the empty fireplace, looking devastated. I had never seen him so upset. He usually looked crushed when his inventions didn't work, which was often enough, but this was different. He had the look of someone who'd been told that an old friend had just died. Like he had tuned the rest of the world out and was just sadly contemplating the meaning of life.

Finally, I sat down next to him. "I don't mean to say that you looked dumb," I said. "Just . . . that you aren't really the kind of guy who can pull off a Mohawk. You're not a punk."

"Hey," he said. "I may not be young anymore, but I get frustrated with society, too. Why shouldn't adults get to lash out? It's not like the world sucks that much less after you grow up."

"I'm sorry, Dad," I said. "But you still have that one patch of hair left. You'll find another way to rebel."

"You mean another way to deal with a midlife crisis," he grumbled. "Maybe I should just buy a sports car like everybody else."

"Come on," said my mother. "You know that won't make you any younger or cooler. And you're not old enough to have a midlife crisis."

"Fine," he said. "Pre-midlife crisis, then. Same difference. I need to take a trip or something. Anywhere. Maybe I can go live in a gutter for a while."

And he sat there, staring off into space and scowling. The poor guy didn't even have the energy to be a Grilling American that night.

Thursday was a big improvement, school-wise. Activity period was just on Tuesday, Wednesday, and Thursday, so when Skills for the Job Market ended that morning, I was able to face history class with a smile, because I had the longest possible amount of time before *more* activity period in front of me.

The day was made all the better by another appearance from Coach Hunter before Coach Wilkins's class.

"Another one!" he moaned. "Will you look at this? This one's downright filthy!"

"Let me see," said Wilkins, taking the sheet. He looked it over and read a couple of lines out loud, then read the rest to himself. "Wow. This is pretty rough," he said. "It's not as bad as the poem it's based on, though."

"Can I see it?" I asked.

Coach Wilkins passed it over to me.

"I'll bet you know what it says already, don't you?" asked Coach Hunter.

"I told you, Coach," I said. "I don't."

I looked down at the poem on the page.

WAIL!

by the Same Guy

I saw the best minds of my generation

destroyed by gym class,

starving, hysterical, sweating, dragging

themselves around

one more lap in fifth period, waiting for the

angry bell.

Who climbed to the top of the rope and cried

"Holy" and studied volleyball, basketball,

dodgeball, while the floor instinctively vibrated

at their feet at the foul line,

who allowed themselves to be made the

subject of paramilitary rage

and wailed with joy when the vein in the

coach's neck twitched

and his eyeball also twitched,

who were awash in a sea of squats squats

squats and rubber balls

and cried out "Rage! Rage!" against the starting

of the class.

Students of the world, I'm with you in gym

class.

I'm with you in gym class,

where we circled in an eternal square dance.
I'm with you in gym class,
where we longed for the days of playing with
parachutes.
I'm with you in gym class,
trying to see up your shorts when you stretch,
checking out your
butt when you present the coach with push-ups.
I'm with you in gym class,
hearing the action-movie music in my head as
the rubber
ball flies toward your head like a missile in the
musky air.
I'm with you in gym class,
where the sad coach wailed the lonely wail that
begged to
become a cry from the grave.

"Not bad," I said. "What's it based on?"

" 'Howl,' by Allen Ginsberg," said Coach Wilkins. "You're lucky, Gene. The original is a lot longer. More obscene, too."

"One more of them, Harris," Coach Hunter said to me. "One more, and it's locker search time. And if I find one obscenity in any of them, it's military school for whoever's writing this stuff!"

I was past worrying about getting my locker raided, of course. I'd already cleared it out enough that all he'd find were some smelly gym socks, which he was welcome to.

But it was a good thing he didn't go on the search right

away. After class, I opened my locker and a piece of yellow paper fell out. I picked it up and saw that it was a note from Jenny.

```
Dear Leon,
    Thanks again for your kind invitation to
become a pirate. Sorry I couldn't do it, but
please don't think it means I'm not crazy
enough or anything. I swear I can keep up
with you guys. I really can. See you at
gifted pool tomorrow.
Break on through,
Jenny


    P.S. Out of curiosity, have you ever seen
a girl naked?
```

I stared at that note—the last line of it, anyway—for a really long time before shoving it in my pocket, where Anna wouldn't see it, and spent the next class trying to get Jenny out of my head, but you don't get a letter with a last line like that and forget about it. Jenny hadn't exactly offered me the chance to see *her* naked or anything. In fact, when I thought about it, I felt as though she could have been a bit more specific. Was she asking if I knew what a naked girl looked like, like from pictures and stuff, or if I had actually seen one myself, in person? 'Cause they're two different things, but she didn't seem to differentiate.

I was awfully glad that I'd gotten it out of my locker, though. If Coach Hunter had found it, he would have passed it on to Dr. Brown. Then he'd know we were plotting some sort of piracy, and I shuddered to think of what sort of videos he'd make Jenny watch to warn her not to write things like that to a guy.

And anyway, if that happened, word of the note would get back to Anna, and I really didn't want to know how she'd react. Maybe she'd get mad at Jenny. Maybe she'd get mad at *me*. If she saw that I'd gotten a letter like that, she'd surely know what I spent the next class period thinking about, after all. Things were already a bit awkward between Jenny and me, not to mention between Anna and me. Something like this couldn't possibly help.

In any case, I was very glad that Jenny had a different lunch period than me. I didn't know if I'd be able to see her without getting either really embarrassed or really turned on, and I didn't want to be either. As usual, though, just having Anna show up took every thought of Jenny out of my head. It worked every time.

At lunch, Anna, Brian, Edie, and I hardly even mentioned the upcoming piracy. Anna was talking about Louis Wain, one of the artists they'd been discussing in the art history activity. He was a guy who painted cats and stuff, and then he went crazy and started painting the cats as crazy, too.

"God, I wish I were in that class," I said. "Know what we talked about in my activity? Resume-writing skills."

"Too bad you couldn't take political science," said Edie. "We argued about free trade all morning—it was awesome! Everyone thought I was crazy!"

"Speaking of crazy," I said, "Coach Hunter is on the warpath."

"Which one did he find?" asked Dustin. "I hid about five of them in his office."

"'Wail,'" I said. "He's threatening a locker raid on everyone in the pool."

"He can't do that!" said Edie.

"Maybe he can, maybe he can't," I said, "but there's nothing saying he won't. Get anything incriminating out of your locker as soon as you can."

"I wish I had some dog crap I could leave in there," said Brian. "Maybe I could make, like, a spring contraption that would throw crap at whoever opens the door without punching in a secret code that only I know or something."

I had no doubt that he could make this work.

"Yeah," said Anna. "But if he never does the search, you're stuck with dog crap sitting in your locker."

"Small price to pay if it might lead to Coach Hunter getting crap in his eye."

Lunch period was a welcome twenty-minute break from thinking about anything of any consequence. Between the upcoming piracy and the whole business with Jenny, the Coach Hunter stuff seemed like an amusing sideshow.

Once lunch was over, though, I was back to thinking about the note in my back pocket. All through the day, I tried my absolute hardest to keep from picturing Jenny naked, but it wasn't easy. And I knew, from having had her sit on me on the couch and stuff, that she was reasonably developed and everything—she probably looked great naked.

So did Anna, though, I kept reminding myself. I tried to picture *her* naked instead, which, in all honesty, was not difficult. But then I'd start picturing both her *and* Jenny naked, and, to make a long story short, it was probably the longest afternoon I'd ever spent in class. I needed to get home. Badly.

But I still waited for Anna outside, just like always, and I walked a lot closer to her than I normally did as we headed to the edge of the parking lot.

"Well," I said, "tomorrow night will be the last planning meeting. We're going to have to get all our stuff in order tonight."

"I'll send everyone an e-mail," Anna said. "See ya tomorrow, sailor."

She started walking away, but I said, "Wait," grabbed her by the arm, pulled her back to me, and kissed her. Hard. And long. With tongue, which was unusual for us. A couple of people shouted out the windows of their parents' cars as they passed by. For a second I was afraid she'd pull away and ask what I thought I was doing, but she didn't.

In fact, she was kissing me back just as hard. She even grabbed the small of my back and started pulling me a little bit closer, but I took a step back so I wouldn't be pressing too much against her. I'd been picturing her naked the whole day. She might have been able to tell.

"Well," she said as she finally pulled away from me. "Something got into you today, huh?"

"You could say that," I said, feeling like I was standing at about a forty-five-degree angle so as not to be up against her.

She smiled and headed away. I ran home as fast as I could.

An hour after I got home, Dad called me downstairs. He sounded pretty happy. Downright chipper, in fact. Clearly, the loss of his Mohawk had not knocked him out for good.

He was wearing all black—black pants, a black turtleneck sweater, and black sunglasses. His scalp was terribly pale, and what was left of his hair was sculpted into one pointy spike, like he had a green horn on the front of his head.

"Um, Dad?" I asked. "Do you know you look like a half-man, half-rhinoceros time traveler from the future?"

"It's the latest style for the hair-free gentleman," he said.

"You seem awfully chipper," I said. "Good day with the dye?"

"Gonna have to let that slide for a couple of weeks," he said. He tapped himself on the head. "I don't have much hair left to test new models on, and after yesterday, I certainly can't imagine you'd want to volunteer as a guinea pig."

"Thanks for guessing that far ahead," I said.

"So," he said, "I figured I'd need something else to pass the time. I took a sick day to figure out how to make this spike and then did some shopping. Come see what I got!"

I followed him out to the garage. The card tables he used for experimenting were folded up along the wall, and all the lab equipment was gone—presumably in the boxes in front of the card tables. In their place, in the center of the garage, where sensible people keep their cars, were a bright red electric guitar and a small amplifier.

"You got a guitar!" I blurted.

"Isn't it a beaut?" he asked.

"What kind is it?" I asked, walking up to it.

"The red kind," he said. He picked it up and turned on the amp. It hummed softly, until he started very sloppily playing the riff from "Smoke on the Water," which is known throughout the land as the easiest song in the world to play badly.

"Does Mom know about this?" I asked.

"Not yet," he said.

"She might kill you," I said.

He stopped playing for a second. "Yeah," he said. "I thought about that. But she didn't kill me over the Mohawk. Lots of guys find themselves sort of at loose ends when they get to my age, you know. Call it a midlife crisis, a pre-midlife crisis, or whatever, it's all the same thing. But it happens to everyone. Some guys get sports cars. Some have affairs with younger women. All things considered, she'll know that starting a rock band probably isn't the worst thing I could do."

"Band?" I said. "You're starting a band?"

"Sure," he said. "No point in getting a guitar if you don't have a band, right?"

"Well," I said, "one could argue that you should learn to play first."

"Hey, man," he said, "it's only rock and roll!"

For a split second, I barely recognized him. This bald man in black with the shades and the green spike frankly didn't look a thing like my dad. And he didn't look any cooler, really.

But he was smiling, at least. If I didn't have the upcoming piracy to remind myself about, I would have been quite worried that my dad, of all people, had become cooler than me. If there was one thing that could've strengthened my resolve as a buccaneer, it was that. I may have been a bit of a dork, but on the worst day of my life, I hoped I would never be a bigger dork than my dad.

Two hours later, there was an e-mail from Anna.

Yo ho ho, mateys!

Tomorrow at Sip during the game will be the last strategy meeting before the takeover. I'll have the map. Troy will be joining us. Don't tell anyone about anything. But have the following items ready:

Nice clothes. We need to look like people who work as accountants (and not the kind who have Mohawks. No offense, Leon).

A stapler. We won't have pistols or daggers, like most pirates, so we should all be packing staplers.

An office accessory. Andy offered to bring a couple of small desks in his car, but we should each bring something else. A piece of boring artwork or a fern or something. Be creative.

All the video gear you have. Remember, this is all for a movie. The only people who are probably going to know about this at all are people who happen to come into Wackfords while we're there, so we won't be making much of a point just by taking over the store. We need the movie to make our point.

```
Wackfords is more of an office than a coffee
shop. Let's show the world, and send them to
Sip.
Anchors aweigh,
Anna
```

I quickly wrote back a message with the subject of "re:
no offense, Leon." The message said

```
     None taken. But the Mohawk is gone—he ac-
cidentally burned it off yesterday. Now he
just has a spike and he's starting a rock
band.
```

Five minutes later, I got a response. At first I thought it
was just one word ("weird!"), but then I scrolled down and
saw she'd added a line at the bottom.

```
     P.S. Out of curiosity, have you ever seen
a girl naked?
```

Oh, God.

Obviously, she must have known about Jenny. Surely
she knew I was refusing Jenny's advances, right?

This could not have been a coincidence. I checked the
note in my back pocket—it was still there; she couldn't
have seen it. But she must have known somehow that
Jenny was sending me notes that said that . . . I knew she
had a class or two with Jenny. Maybe she'd seen her writing it. Did she think the fact that I hadn't told her about

it meant that I was maybe making out with Jenny on the side?

I thought I should write back to Anna right away and confess everything, but I decided against it. After all, I didn't have anything to confess. Sure, I'd gotten a couple of notes, and I'd had trouble keeping from thinking about certain things that day. But there's no rule saying you can't get moderately suggestive notes from someone you aren't dating, right? And anyway, no one had said Anna and I were officially a couple to start with. I had every right to picture anybody I wanted naked.

I didn't sleep a bit that night.

I saw Anna on the way into class the next morning, and, when she saw me, she grinned evilly and pulled some devil horns out of her backpack, then winked as she put them on, which freaked me out a bit. Did this mean she knew something? Or was she just rubbing in the note she'd sent the night before?

I worried about what the heck was going on all morning, until finally, at lunch, when she and I sat down before anyone else had arrived, I asked her about that last line.

"What about it?" she asked, smiling extremely sexily.

"Well," I said, "where did *that* come from?"

She laughed and leaned in really close. "Can you keep a secret?" she asked. I thought I felt her tongue brush against my ear a little bit.

"Yeah," I whispered back.

"Jenny has a crush on someone!" she said. "She won't tell me who, though."

Aha! It was all falling into place. She knew about Jenny, just not what it had to do with me!

"No kidding?" I said, using my ninja skills to play it cool. "So what's the whole thing have to do with seeing a girl naked?"

"She asked me for help writing to the guy," said Anna, "and I suggested she put that at the end. It's not too scandalous; it's not like she's offering the guy a chance to see *her* naked or anything, it's just an honest question. But it's pretty eye-catching, huh?"

"You might say that," I said.

She giggled and kept whispering. "I was so proud of coming up with it that I thought I'd use it on you. It doesn't mean I'm going to get naked for you or anything, but, well . . . how did you sleep last night?"

I blushed. "Not well," I said.

She laughed, pulling away from my ear. "Then my work here is done," she said.

"Do you have any idea who the guy might be?" I asked.

"Nope," said Anna, smiling. "She won't tell me."

"I hope the guy knows how to take the note," I said. "There are guys who might think of that as an invitation, you know."

"She said he'd know how to take it," said Anna. "And come on—it's Jenny. It's probably some guy who's just as sheltered as she is."

"Oh, I don't know," I said. "I think it stands to reason that she'd like some cool, rebellious guy who breaks all the rules and lives like Jim Morrison, don't you think?"

"Nah," said Anna. "She probably likes some guy who's

really good in chemistry class or something. She'd be scared to death of a guy who was really rebellious."

"No, she wouldn't," I said. "She'd think he was bursting with exotic appeal. I'll bet it's some really cool, smart guy."

Twelve hours earlier, her suggestion that Jenny was probably interested in a nerdy sort of guy would have made me feel terrible, but just having solved the mystery of how Anna had known about that last line had me too relieved to care.

Brian and Edie arrived at the table, followed by Dustin and James.

"Shhh," Anna whispered. "Change the subject. She doesn't want anyone else to know."

I was only too happy to oblige.

"One day to go," I said.

"Yeah," said James. "I want you to have this for your takeover." He pulled a stapler out of his backback—a small gray one that looked pretty old. "It's part of my collection."

"It's from Coach Hunter's office?" I asked.

He nodded. *"Mais oui,"* he said. "It's the pride of my collection, but I think it'd be nice for it to be in a movie."

"Thanks!" I said, taking it. "It'll look great with all the business gear."

"I'm not sure about this business gear thing," said Edie to Anna.

"Well, it wouldn't be an office if we showed up in T-shirts," said Anna. "Don't you have anything sort of dressy? Something like an accountant would wear?"

"Just the dress I wore to my great-aunt's funeral," said Edie.

"That'll do," said Anna. "What about you, Brian?"

"I have a button-down shirt," he said. "And a tie."

"Perfect."

Edie rolled her eyes. "I hope this is the only time I see you in them," she said.

"I think I can get a bunch of those lame motivational posters to put up," I said. "My dad has a pretty good supply."

"Excellent," said Anna. "Then we should be all set."

And I felt her move her foot over onto the top of mine, and I was almost certain it wasn't accidental.

I was the first one on the couch at the gifted-pool meeting that afternoon. Edie came in next and sat down near me, but not on me. Then came Marcus, who sat on Edie, and James, who sat on Marcus. Just when I was starting to feel a bit lonely, Anna came in and sat right on my right leg, reclining her back against my chest and face.

Then Jenny arrived, and I just about froze. I'd barely seen her since the cab ride on Saturday, since I didn't have any regular classes with her. But when she saw me with Anna on my lap, she sort of shrank her head into the neck portion of her sweater, like she was a turtle slipping into its shell. Obviously, she was a bit embarrassed.

"Hey, Jenny," said Anna, very friendly-like. "Climb aboard."

"Okay," said Jenny softly, and a bit nervously. But she put her Mountain Dew/Jim Morrrison's Soul bottle on an empty desk, put her coat on a chair, and climbed onto my free knee.

I guess you could say I was conflicted. I didn't *want* to enjoy the feeling of Jenny's butt pressing into my thigh, or the sight of that little bit of bare skin between her pants and her shirt. But on the other hand, I did enjoy it. A lot.

Mr. Streich came in a minute later. "Hi, couch people," he said. "Everybody have a good week?"

We all sort of nodded.

"Making progress on your projects?"

"We are," said Anna.

"Then I yield the floor to Miss Brandenburg," said Mr. Streich.

Anna got off my knee and stood up. "Leon, Brian, Edie, and I are starting principal photography on a filmed monument to the old downtown," said Anna.

"Like the old Venture, Douglas, and Seventieth Street triangle area?" asked Mr. Streich.

"Right," said Anna. "Our film will be a monument to a part of town that may not last much longer in the face of the rising development of the Cedar Avenue business district."

"That's a neat idea," said Mr. Streich. "So you guys don't like Cedar Avenue much, I take it?"

"It sucks!" Edie shouted from underneath a few guys on the couch. It was a weird thing—Brian and Edie were officially a couple, but Edie happily let several guys sit on her on the couch. Anna and I still weren't exactly official, but she only sat on me.

"We feel it has its advantages and disadvantages," said Anna very diplomatically. I liked how she left out certain details, like the main details, of the film. If we'd told him we were going to be taking over the Wackfords as part of the movie, he surely would have nixed the idea.

"Well," said Mr. Streich. "You aren't going to be throwing rocks through the window of the Mega Mart or anything, right?"

"Nothing like that," I said. "Nothing violent."

"Then I hereby approve the project," he said. "Now, if you want to throw a rock through my mother-in-law's window, be my guest."

When class wound up, we all hoisted ourselves up from the couch. Jenny slinked away quickly, without saying a word. She just put on her coat, picked up her soul bottle, and headed out. But when she got to the door, she turned back and smiled in my direction for a split second before turning and walking away.

"Basketball tonight," I said out loud, just to confirm, though we certainly knew that tonight, of all nights, we wouldn't be watching any basketball game. Brian, Edie, and Anna all nodded, and we went our separate ways.

A while after I got home, I heard the sounds of an electric guitar coming loudly from the garage. After a few minutes, I decided maybe he was trying something called "The Damn Song," because all I heard, over and over, was a discordant *chunka chunka* coming out of the guitar, followed by him saying "Damn!" as he hit a bad note. It was pretty excruciating. I was almost relieved when my mother came home, and he came inside to turn from Nicholas Harris: Rock and Roll Accountant, into Lester: Grilling American.

"Yee-haw!" he shouted as he dragged the bag of charcoal to the back porch. "Time to get some vittles a-burnin'!"

"Yeah, you'll burn 'em, all right," said my mother in her Wanda voice. "Burn 'em right to a crisp is what!"

134

"Stifle, woman!" said my father/Lester. "You gotta make sure it's dead, you know!"

"I like mine rare," said Wanda. "I don't even like the cow to be cooked—just scare it a little and bring it on! And real men like it rare, too."

"Can it, Wanda," said Lester, who was pronouncing "Wanda" like "wander." "I know what real men like. And what True Americans do. They grill!"

This would have made another good nature documentary—the domestic habits of imaginary suburban hillbillies. I tried to keep myself from imagining the scene where they wrestled over control of the remote and marked the recliner as their territory, but I was unsuccessful.

As I sat through a whole dinner of this, I started to think I could see the upside of going to prison for taking over the Wackfords. Nobody has ever said anything good about prison food (except for that whole thing about choosing your last meal before they fry your ass), but you probably don't have to watch your parents make fools of themselves while you eat.

Eight o'clock rolled around and Dad drove me out to the basketball game, where I met up with Brian and Edie at the concession stand. Anna arrived a minute later.

"Well," she said, "this could be our last night of freedom if they throw us in jail."

"Hey," said Brian. "If we're in jail at least five months, then today was our last day at Cornersville Middle School."

As the first strains of the national anthem came out of the gym, we were walking out the door toward Da Gama Park. It was cold out, but warmer than it had been the previous few days. My nose didn't feel like it was about to fall off, and I wasn't thinking of saying prayers of thanks to Satan for keeping hell burning and keeping my feet warm. It was a step up.

We marched through Da Gama Park, then down Seventieth Street, with Edie complaining all the way, as usual.

"Damn it, warm up!" she commanded the heavens. "I'm freezing my ovaries off!"

"I think the correct term is 'freezing my ovaries out,' " said Anna.

"They say it's about to start snowing again," said Brian.

There hadn't been new snow in a while—it had actually been too cold for snow to come down for the past couple of weeks. We'd just been trudging through the dirty sludge that was left over from late December.

When we got to Sip, Dustin was sitting there, just relaxing on one of the easy chairs. James was at a table, playing chess with some old guy I didn't recognize. And Troy was sitting at a corner table, wearing sunglasses indoors. He gave us a nod, and we made our way over to his table.

"Ahoy," he said, smiling.

"Hey," I said, sitting down. "Is everything in order?"

"Andy and I are the only ones on the schedule for tomorrow morning," said Troy. "Andy's bringing some office furniture you can use. You guys'll have at least three hours before the boss shows up."

"Three hours?" said Edie. "I was hoping we'd have the run of the place for days."

"That would get you in trouble for sure," Troy said. "You

should be able to get all the footage you need by the time Harold comes in."

Anna pulled a rolled-up sheet of paper out of her coat. "This is the map," she said. "So we can plot how to set up the office."

She unrolled the paper and laid it out on the table. It was an aerial view of the inside of the Wackfords, labeled "Ye Olde Coffee Shoppe." Outside of the drawing was a street, labeled "Cedar Avenue—here there be monsters!"

"Arrr!" said Brian. I'm pretty sure it was an "arrr" of approval.

"We'll get the desk set up here," said Anna. "In front of the main counter. The fern can go in front of the espresso machine."

"I can bring a filing cabinet," said Edie. "Where should it go?"

We all looked at the map for a second. "How tall is the cabinet?" asked Troy.

"Not very," said Edie. "Just, like, two drawers. I have to be able to carry it, you know."

"Then we'll put it on top of the condiment bar to make it look taller."

A minute later, we had a plan pretty well in place. We'd just set up some office gear, take our places, and act very serious and professional the whole time. We'd take turns working the desk and bothering customers, two at a time, while the other two did some filming. It'd probably be hell on wheels to edit it all into something coherent, but even if we only got a few hours of footage from each camera, that'd be a total of six hours' worth of shots—and that was in addition to all the footage we'd need of the old down-town. More than enough to edit into a short film.

"All right," said Anna, rolling up the map. "Everyone's sworn to secrecy from now until tomorrow morning. We'll meet at the Quickway at five. You too, Troy."

"Why Quickway?"

"We'll need you to film us walking down the road to take over the store."

"Fair enough."

So we all shook hands and nodded, then headed back to the high school. We got back right around halftime, which meant we were there for far more of the actual basketball game than normal. I called my dad during the last quarter of the game, and he was one of the first parents to arrive in the parking lot. It was just starting to snow when we pulled into the driveway.

10

What bothers me most about *The Slime That Ate Cleveland* is that I don't understand the main character's motivation. If I were a city-eating slime, I would probably be more inclined to eat Anaheim, California, or Aspen, Colorado. Someplace touristy and clean. Or maybe I'd head to Little Italy in New York, which I assume would be delicious. I would certainly not start anywhere in Ohio.

The night before we took over the Wackfords, *The Slime That Ate Cleveland* was on *The Late Movie with Count Dave* on WOTT, a station loved throughout the entire metro area for its tireless devotion to low-rent crap. On Friday nights, they have this guy called Count Dave who dresses up as a vampire and introduces old horror movies. Before the commercial breaks, he comes on and makes fun of the movie. My dad watches him religiously.

The Slime That Ate Cleveland sucked. Really, really sucked. And not even in that "so bad it's funny" way. The slime just looked like chocolate syrup, the dialogue was boring, and they tended to spend a very long time showing scientists doing experiments that never seemed to end in an explosion. However, I found that it had exactly three redeeming qualities.

Number 1: Saying halfway through that I couldn't sit through it gave me an excuse to go up to bed. My parents had only been watching bits of it while they worked on cleaning out the fridge, but they couldn't blame me. Hence, I was able to get to bed fairly early.

Number 2: The first guy to get eaten by the slime looked a lot like Coach Hunter. In fact, the first guy to see the creature in the movies Count Dave shows almost always looks like Coach Hunter.

Number 3: It gave me a great idea for something to say during the movie. I could describe Cedar Avenue as "The Slime That Ate Cornersville Trace."

Just a few hours later, I was out of bed, showered, dressed in slacks and a button-down shirt, and trying to figure just how the hell one goes about tying a necktie. In the end, I just left it hanging loosely. I wandered downstairs to the closet in the den, where I found Dad's stash of motivational posters. He'd put them all over the house a year or so before, including in the bathroom, but I'd taken them down myself. Every now and then he'd try to sneak a new one up, but I never let them last long. I gathered them up, along with the video camera.

Just before I left, I got Coach Hunter's stapler out of my backpack and slipped it into my pocket.

It was pitch-black out, and remarkably quiet. Most of the time, when I stood in my driveway, I could hear the dull hum of cars on Eighty-second Street or up on Cedar Avenue, but at four o'clock on Saturday morning, the only sound was the wind. Somewhere off in the distance, I thought I heard a train whistle, which must have been coming from a long way away—I didn't know of any train tracks between Cornersville and Preston that were still in use. As I crossed August Avenue, it suddenly occurred to me that this was really the first time I'd been out alone when it was dark. It was a little bit scary, frankly. I mean, everyone knows what to do if a drug dealer comes out from behind a mailbox and offers you some crack, but there are no commercials or after-school specials about what to do in the event of a ghost attack.

I'd only gotten about a block, though, when I heard Anna coming up the road. She was carrying a large fern, and hurried to catch up to me.

"Hey," I said.

"Hey." She smiled. "All set?"

"Everything but the necktie," I said. "I couldn't figure it out."

She giggled and put down the plant. "Here," she said. "I can do it."

She reached out for the zipper of my coat and started unzipping it, and I nearly died. Call me pathetic, but even though it was only my coat, in some small way, Anna, a girl, was undressing me. It was all I could do to stay standing up.

She got my coat undone, grabbed the ends of my tie, started wrapping them around each other, and a few seconds later had them worked into a regular Windsor knot, or whatever you call

141

knots in neckties. Then she pulled the end to tighten it, grabbed it to pull me closer, and kissed me on the nose.

"Where'd you learn to do that?" I asked.

"My mom's in Europe a lot," she said, "and my dad couldn't tie his own tie to save his life."

"You don't kiss his nose, though, right?"

"Nope." She smiled. "I only do that for cute pirates." She kissed it again, then stepped back and said, "Is that a stapler in your pocket, or are you just happy to see me?"

"Stapler," I said. "But I'm happy to see you, too."

Between the wind hitting my cheeks and the blushing, my face must have been as red as my necktie. She picked her plant back up, and we proceeded north toward the Quickway. By the time we got to Cedar Avenue, the snow was coming down pretty hard.

Brian and Edie were at the Quickway already, standing under the lights by the gas pumps in a way that made them look strangely glamorous. Brian, dumbass that he was, wasn't wearing a coat, just a sport jacket over a shirt and tie. Edie was wearing some sort of shawl over a long black dress. They were both shivering. There were another fern and a filing cabinet sitting next to them.

"Avast!" Brian shouted.

"Yo ho ho," I replied as we walked up to join them. Brian grabbed a stapler out of his pocket as though he were drawing a gun and pointed it at me. I pulled Coach Hunter's stapler out of my own pocket and pointed it back at him.

"Careful!" said Edie. "If some cop sees you doing that and thinks it's a gun, he'll shoot you, like, fifty times before you hit the ground!"

"Oh," said Brian, putting the stapler back in his pocket.

"Check out what I brought," said Edie, opening the filing cabinet. She pulled out a sheet of fabric that turned out to be a skull and crossbones pirate flag.

"Perfect!" said Anna. "Someone can wave it as we walk up to the store."

"Any sign of Troy yet?" I asked.

"Nothing so far," said Brian. "You want to go ahead and start filming?"

I nodded, and he pulled out a camera from his bag and turned it on.

He pointed the camera at me first.

"Mr. Harris," he said.

"That's Captain Harris," Anna said with a giggle.

"Fine. Captain Harris, how do you feel?"

Coming up with original questions was clearly not Brian's strong suit.

"Well," I said, "Cedar Avenue is sort of turning into the slime that ate Cornersville Trace. It's been too long since we had a good piracy around here."

He turned the camera to Anna. "How about you, First Mate Brandenburg?"

"Cornersville was designed to have a centralized population," said Anna. "The new downtown and the subdivisions around it are an example of poor city planning at best, and the very thought of replacing Sip with a chain of stores that are more like an office than a coffee shop is a sad cultural loss for the town."

It sounded a little rehearsed, honestly. But it was pretty professional.

He turned over to Edie. "And First Mate Scaduto?"

I wasn't sure you could have two first mates, but I didn't bring it up.

"The revolution is coming," she said. "Soon the people will control the means of production."

I assumed we'd be editing out a lot of Edie's scenes.

Just then, we heard someone shouting "Ahoy!" and turned around to see Troy leaning out the window of an old blue sedan. Andy was sitting in the driver's seat.

"Morning," Troy said, climbing out of the car and walking up to us. "You guys ready?"

"Sure," I said. "Can you follow us and take some shots of us walking up?"

"No problem. Unless I freeze to death."

He took the camera from Brian and walked along backward in front of us as we marched up to the Wackfords, carrying ferns and a filing cabinet. In addition to keeping you from being able to tell whether sandwiches glowed in the dark, the lights in the gas station provided perfect fill lighting for the shots.

Andy drove on ahead, and we trudged down Cedar Avenue through the early-morning snow. I could practically hear marching music playing in my head. It was just four of us, plus a guy with a camera, but I felt like we were an armada closing in on the enemy ship.

As we got up closer to the store, Brian shouted, "Wackfords!" and whacked me in the arm.

"Not anymore it isn't," I said. And we all socked him back—that's one of the rules of the Wackfords game. If someone calls out "Wackfords" when there isn't one in sight, everyone present gets to whack that person.

And there wasn't a Wackfords—it was *our* place now. An office. As we walked past the sign and cut into the parking lot, I waved the skull and crossbones high.

In the parking lot, Andy was waiting for us, standing beside the open trunk of his car. "Check it out," he said. "I got you two card tables and a watercooler."

"Card tables?" Anna asked. "Will they look all right as desks?"

"Sure," said Andy, "I have some tablecloths to cover them up with. They'll look decent, and you can pack 'em up and leave pretty quickly if you have to."

"Sweet."

Brian and I helped unload all the gear from the back of Andy's car, which sported a bumper sticker that said I'VE WORKED EVERYWHERE, MAN. Then Troy filmed Edie running the skull and crossbones up the flagpole attached to the building near the door.

"I claim this vessel to be the property of the HMS Pirate Ship," she declared. This was exciting stuff—I'd never taken over a building before! Few among us have, I imagine, and even fewer have done so in a bloodless coup.

We waited around on the patio for a minute or so, filming more shots of the flag waving in the snow, while Andy got the store unlocked and shut off all the security thingies; then we boarded the vessel, as it were. Brian and I set up the card tables right in front of the main counter, and Edie set the filing cabinet on top of the condiment bar. Then Anna and I erected the watercooler right next to it. I loved that we had a watercooler. We could gather around it and talk about television.

The ferns were set up in front of the desks, which helped a lot to create the office effect. Then I unrolled the motivational posters and put them up to cover anything that had the Wackfords logo. Over the menu board behind the counter, I put up a poster that showed a pebble falling into the water, underneath which were the words A SMALL THING MAKES A BIG DIFFERENCE. It didn't look remotely out of place; I could see a day coming when Wackfords would be making their own line of motivational posters to put up in the stores.

In all of fifteen minutes, we were done. We pulled a couple of chairs over to set up behind the desks, and the takeover was complete.

It didn't look much like an accounting and midlevel management strategies office, in all honesty. It looked more like a Wackfords with some new posters on the wall and some tables set up. I figured we could make it look better during editing.

"All right," said Troy, handing the camera to me. "We'd better get the store set up for real."

"You can't!" said Edie. "We've taken you over!"

"Yeah," said Troy. "But we've gotta get the machines fired up and the pastries unwrapped anyway, so we can serve the people who make it past you guys. Unless you're threatening our lives or something. Are you?"

I shook my head. "Nah." I knew we couldn't halt sales completely, after all.

"Okay," said Troy. "You guys want some coffee, or what?"

"No way!" said Edie. "We can't drink Wackfords coffee!"

"Oh, come off it!" said Anna. "You won't die. It's not poison."

"It's not like I'm asking you to pay for it," said Troy. "You can say you plundered it."

"Just as long as nobody has any of it on camera," I said. "Stash your cups out of sight."

"Arr!" said Brian.

I didn't care where it came from—it was five in the morning. I wanted coffee. The fact that we had it in plentiful supply was awfully convenient.

I wandered around, getting some establishing shots. The snow was still coming down hard outside, and the snow directly in front of the store glowed green from the light in the Wackfords sign. Off in the distance, the blue Mega Mart sign shone like some sort of lighthouse.

"Well, now what?" asked Edie while the coffee brewed. "When do you guys open?"

"About half an hour," said Andy. "When you open, the first hour is usually about the same ten people every day, but it's different on Saturday, especially when it's snowing. We won't get many people this morning. No one's on their way to work, they're just going to the mall, and that's not open until ten. We'll pick up in the early afternoon, when they're done shopping, if the snow isn't too bad."

"Well, that's just as well," said Anna. "If we don't have too many people to deal with, we can focus more on making the movie."

"But we have to make every customer count," I said. "Every scene has to be good. We should end up agonizing over what we have to take out, not just patching together a few good scenes."

When the coffee was ready, I drank mine black, which I was starting to get used to doing. It did seem oddly, well, *fancier* than the Sip stuff—not as much of the metallic taste of the coffee urn, and not as earthy. I didn't like it as much, either, but it woke me up, which was the important thing. Even Edie sipped hers, though she loaded it up with organic milk. Brian used heavy cream and about half a bottle of hazelnut syrup.

"Okay," I said. "We'll be open in fifteen minutes, so let's do a quick review. Anyone comes in and asks for a drink, we tell them we just do accounting and management strategies here."

"All right," said Troy. "But if they still want a drink—and they will—I'll make it for them."

"Don't be a pussy, man!" said Edie.

"I'm just saying, is all," said Troy. "You guys can bug them all you want, then I'll bug them a bit if they get past you, but if they still want something, I have to sell it to them."

Edie sulked a bit.

"Don't worry," said Andy. "Even if they get past you guys, I'll give 'em some more trouble."

I filmed Andy making the coffee—he kept getting that bugged-out serial killer look in his eyes and chuckling while he did it, like it was giving him some sort of real thrill to make the coffee. Then he abruptly stopped the chuckling and started whistling "Big Rock Candy Mountain." He was a weird guy, that Andy.

When he was done whistling, I asked Andy to explain what being a McHobo was all about for the camera.

"It's about being bigger than the lousy job," he said. "About finding the dignity in an undignified life. And pretending there's something noble about working for lousy pay. Or at least not letting the overpaid jerks from corporate get you down. Most of these places want you to base your whole life around the job. I've seen people quit school, break up with significant others . . . just wreck their lives over these retail and restaurant gigs. McHobos don't let that happen to themselves."

"Are there a lot of other McHobos in town?" I asked.

"Practically everyone working on Cedar Avenue could be one," he said. "Most of them just don't realize it. There are only a few of us who really get into the whole culture, but the number is growing just as fast as the strip malls go up. And those who don't embrace the McHobo code will follow the rules, get a raise, get promoted, and end up stuck in one of these lousy joints until they rot."

Outside, dawn was breaking over the retail wasteland. There was no sun in sight, just snow that was falling harder and harder, but it wasn't as dark.

Edie told Brian to follow her outside with the camera, and she stood out in the middle of the empty, snowy street and stuck up her middle finger at the Wackfords sign. Then she gracefully turned to the side and flipped off the Burger Box sign. Then she arched her back and pointed her middle finger up at the Mega Mart sign, which loomed large above all the others. She slowly turned around, sticking up both middle fingers at the whole street, then, slowly, began to wave both hands around, like she was conducting an orchestra with her middle fingers while the white snowflakes stuck to her black shawl and her black and red hair. Brian filmed the whole thing.

Ten minutes later, the store opened and we got our first customer.

I must admit that I was nervous as hell when Troy unlocked the door at six o'clock. I mean, there was nothing to guarantee that the first guy in the door wasn't going to be a cop who hated commies and wanted to make an example out of Edie by taking her downtown for breaking in to the store. And he might take us all with her.

But the first customer was a guy dressed in khaki pants, a denim shirt, and a tie. He must have been at least in his midforties, but he had a dark tan, probably a spray-on, seeing as how it was January, and his hair was frosted. He looked as though he thought that he was pretty hot shit, even though he was probably a yes-man. He probably didn't realize that his hair was thinning, though we could tell from the store when he was still in the parking lot.

"Oh, perfect," said Troy as the guy walked up to the door from his SUV. "It's Johnny B. Important. You guys are gonna *love* him."

We all took our places as the guy came inside. Anna and I were starting out sitting at one of the "desks," and Edie and Brian stood off to the side, filming everything.

"Grando nonfat latte," the yes-man muttered, without so much as a hello, before he was even at the counter. He took no notice of the desks or the cameras.

"Sorry, sir," I said from behind the desk. "We don't serve lattes here."

"Come on," he said. "I have to be in the city in an hour, and you're going to make me late."

"I'm terribly sorry," said Anna. "But there's been a corporate takeover. We just do accounting and midlevel management strategies here."

"What the hell is this?" the guy asked Andy.

"We've been taken over by pirates," said Andy. "If you order a drink, you may have to face the wrath of the crew."

Anna grabbed a few of the surveys she'd brought and handed them to him. "You're welcome to stay, but we'll need you to get started on this paperwork right away. If you want a regular coffee shop, try Sip on Venture Street."

"Do you guys have any idea who I am?" the guy asked. I didn't know people actually asked that question.

"Yes, sir, you're a man who schedules important meetings on the weekend," said Anna. "If you need to know more than that, perhaps you could try asking the police."

"Or the FBI," said Edie from behind the camera. "They have files on everybody!"

The guy looked over at Troy and Andy. "Will one of you *please* make me a goddamned grando nonfat latte before I have you both fired?"

"We don't sell goddamned lattes," said Andy. "Only holy, sanctified ones. Would you care for one of those?"

"Whatever. Just give me a drink."

Troy made the guy a latte, and the guy muttered a few things that he probably didn't say out loud in front of his mother and stormed off, saying something about calling the guy on the news who does consumer reports or something.

"That was about the friendliest I've ever seen that guy," Andy remarked.

"That schmuck's in here all the time," said Troy. "There's no way he's got an important meeting. I mean, it's Saturday. He's probably off to let his boss beat him at racquetball."

I suddenly got a bit concerned. "This won't get you in too much trouble, will it, Troy?" I asked. "I don't want you to end up on one of those TV news exposés."

Troy shrugged. "We can get out of it," he said.

"And if there's trouble, I'm taking the blame, anyway," said Andy. "And ol' Johnny B. Important is too busy having meetings and stuff to bother calling in a complaint. Plus, if a customer swears at you, you don't have to be nice to them anymore."

"I'm guessing that's not in the manual," I said.

"Nope. Just the McHobo code. Harold would probably have us give the jerk a formal apology or something. But customers don't get away with that bullshit on my watch."

"How'd that turn out?" Anna asked Brian, who had filmed the proceedings.

"Got some good shots," said Brian. "He didn't end up going to Sip, though."

"Places!" Edie shouted. "Here comes another one!"

An older guy was approaching the door, dressed in business-casual gear: a button-down shirt, slacks, and loafers. He carried a briefcase. He looked around when he came in, and seemed to nod with approval at the motivational posters.

"Morning," said Andy.

"Morning, Andy," he replied. "Nice new look."

"We've changed our image," said Edie. "Instead of being a coffee shop, we're now focusing on accounting and mid-level management strategies."

"Oh yeah?" asked the guy, smiling. "Can I still sit here?"

"Sure," I said. "Especially if you're doing accounting or management strategizing."

"How about finance?" asked the guy. "Is that allowed?"

"Sure," I said. "That's close enough. Welcome to the office."

He nodded. "Can I still have some coffee?"

"Coming right up," said Andy. "On the house." He poured him a cup, and the guy took it over to a table in the corner, opened up his briefcase, and got to work.

I stared over at him from the main desk. We'd just told the guy Wackfords had turned from coffee shop to office, and he'd barely flinched. In fact, he thought it was a good idea.

The experiment was a success already.

"It worked," I muttered to Anna.

"Way too well," she said. "There's no way he really believes us."

"He's playing along," Andy said, leaning over. "He's an okay guy. Comes in every day."

Anna reached under the table and pulled out a stack of the surveys she'd worked up, then walked over to him. By this time, the guy was busy talking on his cell phone, so he barely looked up, and certainly didn't protest, when she said, "Here, we'll need you to get on these right away." The guy smiled and nodded. Brian, of course, got it all on film.

Five minutes went by before anyone else showed up; the snow was falling hard enough that it looked as though we might actually have a blizzard on our hands, which meant that people would be staying inside.

The next person in was a woman who, according to her name tag, worked at the gym down the street. She was wearing sunglasses and looked maybe one-third awake.

"We don't sell coffee anymore," I said as she walked up to the counter. She ignored me completely.

"Mocha," she said to Andy.

"What size?" asked Andy.

"The big one."

"You want extra cheese?"

"No," she said, not awake enough to catch the joke.

"How about fries? You want fries with that?"

"No."

"What if I told you we'd been taken over by pirates and couldn't sell you anything?"

"Whatever. Can I have a mocha?"

"If you insist."

While Troy made the drink, Anna walked up to her and tried to ask her to do some paperwork or something office related, or to get her to go to Sip, but she was pretty unresponsive. She walked out without giving us one decent thing we could put into the movie.

She was followed by a woman who appeared to be about

forty. We went through the routine of telling her Wackfords had been taken over, and she responded with a lecture on how she expected to be treated as a customer, then threatened to call the guy on the news who does consumer watchdog segments if she didn't get her latte for free. Troy gave her one, but she was still mad when she left.

"You get those threats about the news a lot?" I asked. "That's already two today."

"Almost every day," said Troy. "Even when we haven't been taken over by pirates. People think it really makes us shake in our boots or something. Some guy on TV apparently did a story once that said if you threaten a clerk and make a big stink, they'll do anything you want for you. And if I ever find out who it was, I'll punch his lights out."

"It's cute how they think retail clerks really care about them." Andy giggled. "As though the guy making just over minimum wage is going to be *more* concerned about their well-being if they act all whiny and mean. They don't realize how easy it is for me to give them decaf."

"You really do that?" I asked.

"Affirmative." He nodded. "You can't give someone regular if they ask for decaf, because that isn't safe, and violating a customer's safety is against the code. But if you downgrade someone, they'll never be the wiser until they fall asleep at their desk. And they can't prove anything. Let's see 'em call the consumer reporter guy and say that Wackfords violated their right to be an asshole."

"Is it true that waiters spit in your food if you're mean to them?" asked Brian.

Andy smirked. "Of course. And when I delivered pizza, if people didn't tip me, I'd steal things out of their gardens, or eat the toppings off their pizza next time I brought them one."

"Didn't you ever get in trouble?" I asked.

"Nah," he said. "McHobos never worry about getting in trouble."

"Well," I said, "they do say that if you make yourself invaluable, there's no limit to what you can do."

Andy laughed. "I'm not invaluable," he said. "I just don't plan on sticking around long enough for it to matter. For McHobos, there's always another job, and no need to put the current one on your resume."

The customers came in slowly after that. We switched spots now and then, but Brian and Edie weren't as good at dealing with customers as Anna and I were, so we usually switched back pretty quickly.

Then, just before seven-thirty, something we hadn't counted on happened—a person we recognized arrived: Mrs. Smollet, the former director of the gifted pool who had resigned shortly after suspending me over *La Dolce Pubert*.

We recognized her as soon as she stepped out of her car in the parking lot.

"Oh shit," said Brian. "The Wicked Witch of the Midwest."

"I haven't seen her since she resigned," I said, suddenly getting nervous. If anyone was going to call the cops on us, it would be her.

"She comes in from time to time," said Troy.

"You could have told us!" I said.

"I figured you might have guessed," said Troy. "Half the people in town come in from time to time."

"Shh!" said Anna. "Places!"

I sat in my spot at the desk and watched as she came in the door.

"Good morning," I said cheerfully.

Mrs. Smollet looked at me like a church lady who'd just noticed that there was a naked person standing on the altar, then scanned the room, scowling.

"Well, hello, Leon," she said, sounding about as friendly as a pit bull. "Working on another avant-garde film?"

"Something like that," I said, nodding.

"Got the whole gang here, I see," she said.

"We've taken over the Wackfords," said Anna matter-of-factly. "The entire operation is under our control."

"I'm sure," she said. She looked up at Andy and Troy. "Can I get some coffee?"

"Coming up," said Troy.

There was a second or so of very awkward silence. She didn't say anything, and neither did anybody else. Then, for some reason, she went for small talk.

"I suppose they're going to let you go on to high school this fall?" she asked me, making it clear by her tone that she thought this would be a huge mistake.

"As far as I know," I said.

"Well," she said not at all pleasantly, "we can't wait to have you."

Without even making eye contact, she gave me a look that was identical to the one Coach Hunter gave me when he was planning to make my life miserable in gym class.

"Is this the kind of project Max Streich is giving you?" she asked. "Acting like terrorists-in-training?"

"Terrorist?" I asked. "What kind of underachieving terrorist starts out by taking over a place in Cornersville Trace?"

"It's to help us get a good job later," Anna explained. "In today's job market, we need interesting things on our resumes. So we're proactively thinking outside the box. I can assure you that we're not being value neutral here, we've just determined that coffee isn't delivering the wow factor, and that Wackfords needed to restructure if they were to keep on doing the heavy lifting for their valued guests. As pirates, we've done the job for them."

"Everywhere I've worked, they want us to call customers 'guests,'" said Andy with a sneer. "You know what I call them?"

"What?" asked Mrs. Smollet.

"Idiots," said Andy as he handed her a cup of coffee.

She gave him a dirtier look than the one she'd given me.

"Well," she said, "then I suppose this idiot will be on her way. I'll see you this fall, Leon."

"I'm counting the days," I said. And she walked out the door.

"Well," said Anna. "We've annoyed a few customers and irritated Mrs. Smollet. I'd say we're a success already."

Of all the people in Skills for the Job Market, I would be the only one who could put "successful pirate" on my resume.

After surviving a Mrs. Smollet encounter, my confidence went way up. I was fearless, ready to call any customer who came in any dirty name that popped into my head, and eager to force them at sword point to go to Sip and leave the new downtown forever, under penalty of walking the plank. We really should have brought a plank.

By eight o'clock, though, a weird thing had happened. The customers had stopped showing up. Troy and Andy said that after the first hour or so, Saturdays were usually sort of dead until the early afternoon, and, with the snow falling as hard as it was, it was a wonder that we'd had as many customers as we had. People tended to stay home at least until the snowplows came through.

So we'd had probably less than a dozen customers, and given the weather, there was a good chance we wouldn't get many more. The snow looked like it was nearly ankle deep already. We knew our time was short, so we took advantage of the free time by filming shots of us acting like business-people. One person would hold a camera while the rest of us stood around by the watercooler or ran frantically around with the sheets of paper, shouting, "Don't touch my stapler!" Anything to make the place seem more like a typical corporate office.

Of course, none of us really knew what went on in corporate offices, but this was how we imagined it.

Every now and then, I'd pretend to push a button on my desk, and say, "Helen, I need you to order me some more erasers and a package of gummed reinforcements, please." Brian was into yelling, "Where the hell is my donut?" Anna found a rubber stamp that was used to stamp "Frequent Coffee Drinker" cards and started to stamp all the pieces of paper she could find. It was fun, in a sort-of kind-of way. More fun than actually working in an office probably is, anyway.

At one point I walked over to the watercooler, poured myself a cup of water, and stood there. The guy who had been first to use the place as an office came over to talk to me. He'd been in the corner the whole time, working on finance or whatever he was doing.

"So, what's this all about, really?" he asked as he poured himself a cup, too. "Are you guys all working for Sip Coffee? I keep hearing you plug them."

I decided that, if only because it was the easiest thing to remember, I should just tell the truth.

"It's an experiment," I said. "We're seeing if anyone can tell the difference between Wackfords and an accounting office. Can you?"

He shrugged and chuckled a bit. "Not really. I don't go to regular coffee shops. They're full of weirdos all the time, not just when they get taken over by pirates."

I laughed as he took a sip of water.

"I mean, I don't come here for poetry readings, or to discuss politics or anything," he continued. "I'm here to get my work done."

"They don't have poetry readings to start with," I said.

He nodded. "Exactly." He finished his water and said, "Is this some kind of science project, then?"

"Something like that," I said. "It's for school."

He smiled. "I've been watching you guys," he said, "I finished my work a while ago, but I don't want to leave till the snow dies down. You sure the manager isn't gonna call the cops on you?"

"Nope," I said. "It's the risk one runs as a pirate."

"I'm taking the rap," said Andy from behind the counter. "I'm getting fired. Moving on."

"No kidding?" said the guy. "I always hear this is supposed to be a great place to work."

Andy shrugged. "I've had worse. But benefits and open-door policies don't mean a thing if the manager is a loser."

"So Harold's a loser?"

"Well, ya just said it," said Andy with a smile, "and the customer is always right."

"Yeah, he kinda seems like a loser, now than you mention it. The man acts like he has a stick up his butt the size of a goalpost."

I took a seat next to Anna behind the table while Andy and the finance guy discussed Harold's various shortcomings.

"Nice guy," I said. "I think this is going well so far."

"Yeah," she said. "I didn't think it would be this easy. We got rid of Smollet, and we're still in control of the vessel. Nothing but smooth sailing!"

Just then, the door opened and Jenny Kurosawa walked in.

"Hey!" said Anna. "You made it!"

Jenny smiled, though she looked a bit exhausted and almost totally frozen. It was a long, long walk from Oak Meadow Mills. "How's it going?" She looked like she was trying to smile but couldn't move her lips.

"Piece of cake so far," I said. "Andy, get the young lady some hot coffee, please. She's walked clear out here in a snowstorm."

"Right away, Cap'n," said Andy, pouring her some.

Jenny took it and sipped it greedily; then, to my great surprise, and to Anna's as well, from the look of things, she came around the table and sat on my lap.

"Um, Jenny," I said, "you might wanna not do that. I mean, you're holding hot coffee."

"Oops," she said cutely, and stood up in front of the desk.

It was too late, though. I could feel myself, you know, responding to having had her butt on my lap, and with it came that awful feeling of guilt I'd had ever since she'd first kissed me in the cab. I wasn't supposed to feel that sort of stirring about girls other than Anna—I didn't even want to!

"You walked all the way out here from Oak Meadow Mills?" Brian asked. "Are you insane?"

"Yeah," she said, sipping her coffee and smiling. "I just had to see you guys in action. Especially since I knew Leon wanted me to be here."

"Um, Anna," I said, unable to keep my mouth shut any longer. "Let's talk in the back for a second. Filming stuff."

And she followed me to the back room, which was a tiny place featuring a little desk, a large walk-in cooler, a sink, an ice machine, and a whole bunch of crates full of coffee cakes and stuff.

"You know that letter you helped Jenny write?" I asked, summoning every nerve in my body. "The one that said 'Have you ever seen a girl naked?' at the bottom?"

"Yeah." She grinned. "But you *know* I'm not about to get naked in the back room of a Wackfords in the middle of a piracy."

"I know, I know. But, um . . . I think you should know that the letter was to me."

Anna paused for a second, and I stood frozen, ready for her to slap me for not telling her right away, then go out to murder Jenny. Or, equally bad, she could say, "Oh! Well, you and I aren't going anywhere—you should go out with her!" But then, after that horrible second, she laughed out loud.

"Oh, God!" she said in this half groan, half laugh thing. "I guess I should have known. It's not like I haven't noticed her putting her butt on your arm on the couch!"

"You knew about that?" I asked.

"Well," she said, smirking but looking slightly bashful, possibly for the first time in her life. "She's not the only one, you know. You can't fool me with my own tricks!"

"So you aren't mad or anything?"

She laughed again. "Leon," she said, "I can't blame her for liking you! I mean, what's not to like?"

It's weird how Anna could make me feel like a total

dork, or a complete asshole, or the luckiest guy in the world, all in the same day, on many occasions. She never stopped surprising me. Something about her ability to laugh and groan with one sound made me wonder which she meant to do sometimes.

"But . . . she kissed me!" I said.

"Really?" asked Anna, suddenly raising an eyebrow. "Did you kiss her back?"

"No. She sort of surprised me," I said.

She started giggling again. "Poor Jenny. You're probably the first guy she ever liked, and she has no idea what to do."

"Well, you know," I said, "she was asking me what the deal with us is, and I couldn't really say for sure. I mean, we've never said we're, you know . . ."

Anna smiled and grabbed me by the hand. "Sorry," she said. And she sort of half chuckled. "I thought it went without saying. But I forget how badly you suck at telepathy."

And she kissed me on the nose again. I kissed her back, on the lips.

"Come on," she said, chuckling again and bringing me back down to earth. "We have to go be pirates a while longer before the boss shows up."

And we went back out, holding hands. Jenny looked a bit crestfallen when she noticed that, but Anna and I ignored it as well as we could. Or I did as well as I could, anyway. I have to admit that I sort of felt bad for her. But right about then, I was mostly feeling good for myself.

As we started straightening the bits of the "office" that had gotten messed up, Anna asked Jenny how her letter had gone over—without even hinting that she knew who it was for.

"Not very well," said Jenny, looking sort of sad.

"That's too bad," said Anna.

"Well," said Jenny. "I guess I'll just have to keep trying."

"If at first you don't succeed," said Anna.

I'd been worrying my head off about what Anna would say if she found out, and about what she really thought about me. And she'd handled it all like a regular pro.

Jenny sat down in one of the nice chairs near our water-cooler and kept staring at me. Anna leaned over and whispered, "Looks like I have some competition!" in my ear.

"Nothing wrong with some friendly competition," I said.

She chuckled again and whispered, "Yeah, and I won't be easily beaten. But be nice to Jenny. You're probably her first crush."

"Not counting Jim Morrison," I whispered back.

"True. But he's dead, so he doesn't really count."

Anna walked over to the chair where Jenny was sitting and handed her my camera. "Here," she said. "Hang on to this for a second."

"Are you sure?" Jenny asked.

"Yeah," said Anna. "Your parents won't be able to see you if you stay behind a camera!"

"I don't know," said Jenny. "They might hear my voice, or wonder who was doing the filming if all four of you are in the shot."

"Hey, you're here already," said Anna. "Might as well be hanged for a sheep as a lamb."

Jenny sat still for a second, then slowly started to smile. "Break on through," she said, holding the camera up to her eye.

Anna walked back behind the desk and said, "I need all crew members to report for a very important business meeting behind the counter."

Brian, Edie, and I walked over to the counter, and Jenny walked over to film us. Anna walked over to ask the guy who was doing finance if he wanted to attend the meeting, but he smiled and politely waved her off.

"Aw, come on!" Andy said. "Join us!"

"Nah," said the guy. "Any of you guys ever been to a business meeting? They're usually really boring."

"I'll make sure this one is no exception," said Anna.

Anna smoothed her dress, cleared her throat, and began to spout off some business nonsense.

"MaxEdgeCorp is laying off about five hundred employees, according to the rumors," she said, with a totally straight face, "and their stock has just about doubled, probably because they finally fired Jack Preston as acting president and brought in Frank Zappa's corpse; that ought to be a good sign, if you look at his track record with OmniEdge. Now, in regards to the drop-off in the holiday figures and the estimates, I'd say . . ."

The door opened, and a middle-aged woman wearing a green coat over a tacky green outfit came in. She looked like an evil version of my elementary school librarian. The wind slammed the door shut behind her.

"You guys better have coffee!" she shouted.

"Those first five hundred are just the beginning, you

know," I said, ignoring her and playing along with Anna. "It'll push the stock up enough that you can take the wife and kids to dinner, but if you really want the windfall, wait until the third quarter, at least."

The lady in the tacky suit was standing at the counter now, saying "Excuse me!" rather loudly. Clearly, she was not a fan of the "inside voice," which my elementary school librarian never shut up about.

Andy turned toward her, glaring.

"*Excuse* me," he said, "but we're trying to hold an important business meeting right now. We can't be disturbed."

"Excuse *me*," the woman barked, "but I'd like to order a triple mezzo nonfat caramel latte."

"We don't sell those," said Anna. "We just do accounting and midlevel management strategies here. Now if you'll excuse us, we're in the middle of a meeting!" She then went right back to talking, without missing a beat.

"The third quarter will indeed be very interesting," she said, all business. "Once the merger goes through they're gonna be swimming in money over there. So you're right, you should wait to sell, but buy now before more of the layoffs go through. Now, on to the matter of borrowing against equities . . ."

The woman finally threw up her hands. "Will one of you hooligans just make me a drink?" she asked.

"Lady," said Andy, "that sounded like age discrimination. Don't make me send you to cultural sensitivity training!"

"Don't make *me* call your boss," said the woman to Andy. "I can have you fired. I know you're not allowed to let kids behind the counter."

"Call away," said Andy. "I'm getting fired today anyway."

"To conclude our meeting," said Anna, interrupting, "business is good. Meeting adjourned."

"There. Thanks for waiting," said Andy to the woman. "Now, do you want a drink?"

"You know what?" she said. "I don't!"

And she turned on her heel and walked out of the store, as though she'd just had the last word. As the door slammed shut behind her, I heard her shouting "Good gravy!" at the snowy heavens.

"Well," said Andy, "she certainly showed me." He and Troy laughed.

"Man, I hate that lady," said Troy. "She always makes us remake the drink four or five times before it's good enough."

Brian took his camera to the window and filmed the tacky lady getting back into her car.

"You wanna pack it in while we're still ahead?" I asked. "I'd say we've already had a pretty successful takeover. We have more than enough footage."

"Maybe we should," said Anna. "Jenny? What do you think?"

Jenny shrugged, and I noticed she was zooming in on my face. Probably had been for some time. "Maybe you should," she said.

"Um, not yet," said Brian. "Look who's here."

I turned toward the door and saw Coach Hunter walking across the parking lot.

13

"Oh man," said Troy. "I remember that guy."

"I don't believe this," I said. "First Mrs. Smollet, and now this jerk?"

"Who is it?" asked Andy.

"It's the middle school gym teacher," Troy told him. "I'll decaf him."

"Places!" shouted Anna. She and I got into the chairs behind the desks, Brian picked up his camera, and Edie got mine back from Jenny, who smiled and headed back to the booth in the corner. Coach Hunter walked in the door and was clearly surprised to see us.

"What's going on here?" he asked as kicked the snow off his boots.

"Wackfords has been taken over by pirates," Anna explained, "and is now an accounting and midlevel management strategies office."

He stared ahead for a second, not saying anything, with

that confused look he always got when confronted with a problem that could not be solved with push-ups.

"You want a drink?" Andy asked him. "On the house."

"Yes, please," he said. "I don't know what's going on in this town anymore!"

"I'm sorry to hear that," said Andy, who was polishing a bottle of syrup and sort of looking like a bartender. "Want to talk about it?"

Coach Hunter stepped around behind the desks and put his elbow up on the counter with a sigh. "I work down at the middle school, coaching gym for these kids," he said, indicating us. "In the past week, some lousy kid has slipped thirteen nasty poems about how much it sucks to be a gym teacher into my office. And I'm certain that these punks know who it was."

"I keep telling you we don't!" I said.

"My friend," said Andy, "you're talking to a man who knows all about bad jobs. I've had plenty of them."

"I thought I'd come into the coffeehouse," Coach Hunter continued, "sit back and relax for a while, and maybe ask around, see if anyone knows anything. I mean, it's a coffee shop, all the artistic kids probably hang out here on the weekend, right? So I drive out here through a blizzard, and what do I find? More students, taking the place over and saying it's an office now. I just can't get a break! And I'm on to you, Harris!" He pointed at me.

"It's not polite to point," I said.

"Harris!" he barked. "Drop and give . . ." He paused. Obviously, he couldn't order me to do push-ups outside of school, but trying to do so was a reflex. Without being able to fall back on his instincts, he was at a loss for words.

"Well," said Andy, "I'm sorry to hear that. What would you care to drink? Anything you like is on us."

He looked over at me, as if to say "Let this one go," and I nodded. Poor Coach Hunter really did seem to be at the end of his rope. I imagined him leaning on the counter, downing shots of coffee and slurring things like "I do push-ups better when I've had a few!"

He was also, I noticed, the first person who came in thinking Wackfords was a cool coffeehouse where artists hung out. I could see the slogan now: "Wackfords Coffee: Your Gym Teacher Thinks It's Pretty Hip."

"I'll try a cappuccino," said Coach Hunter.

"Sure," said Andy. "Troy, make the good man a double."

"Sure thing," said Troy.

Troy got to work making it, and Coach Hunter looked down at the desk.

"That stapler looks familiar," he said.

"Well," I said, "many staplers look alike, I guess."

He grunted a bit, then looked out the window.

"Leon," said Anna. "Look outside!"

Out in the parking lot, a familiar van—my parents'— was pulling in, and I could see my dad's mostly bald head at the wheel.

"What in the fresh, green hell?" I said. "I didn't know he even came to Wackfords!"

"Maybe he was looking for another place to do some slam dancing," said Anna.

"At Wackfords?" I asked. Then I shook my head for a second. It really did make sense—if there was anybody who thought Wackfords would be a really groovy place to rock out, it would be my dad.

He did a bit of a double take when he opened the door and saw me. I smiled sheepishly.

"Leon!" he said. "Your note said you were out doing stuff for your monument."

"We are," I said. "It's sort of a weird monument."

He looked at me suspiciously for a second. "I guess it must be," he said. "I didn't think you liked Wackfords."

Right about then, Troy called out, "Mezzo cappuccino," and put a cup on the counter. Coach Hunter picked it up, took all of a single sip, and made a nasty face.

"Where's the drink?" he said. "This is a cup of foam!"

"That's a cappuccino," said Andy. "It's two shots of espresso, a dash of milk, and a whole lot of foam."

"The cappuccinos at the Quickway aren't like that!" he grumbled.

"Hey, dude," said my dad, chuckling. "This isn't the gas station! Get hip!"

Coach Hunter frowned at him, and I knew I had to break up the conversation before Dad found out that Coach Hunter knew who I was. He'd surely ask how I was doing in gym class.

"What are you doing here, anyway?" I asked Dad.

"I'm meeting Mr. Streich here in a few minutes," he said. "I'm going to talk to him about being in my rock band."

"Mr. Streich is coming here?" I asked.

"Yeah," said Dad. "I thought he'd be here by now, in fact. Guess the snow slowed him down."

"Oh crap," Anna muttered. And she got up, grabbed me by the arm, and dragged me back into the back room.

"We've got to call it a day," she said. "If Streich finds out exactly what we're doing, there's no way he'll let us use it as our project."

"He might," I said. "He'll probably think it's funny."

"Yeah, but it also might be a felony, or at least a misdemeanor," said Anna. "If there's any evidence whatsoever that he knew about it ahead of time, he'll be fired for sure."

Just then, Andy stuck his head around the corner.

"Minor problem," he said. "King Harold's chariot just arrived." He made a little trumpet noise.

"The boss?" Anna asked.

"Don't worry," I said. "We were just about to pack things up."

McHobos look for signs to tell them it's time to move on, according to Andy. If Mr. Streich, my dad, and the boss showing up at the same time wasn't a sign for pirates to give up the ship, I didn't know what was.

We ran out from the back, quickly told Brian and Edie what was going on, and started cleaning up as fast as we could.

I went on a mad dash around the store, tearing down the motivational posters, while Anna got the watercooler and filing cabinet away from the condiment bar. Brian and Edie got started folding up the tables. I just barely managed to get the last poster down before Harold, who was a lanky guy with mustache and a hairline that had receded its way to his neck, walked in. He looked a bit like an older, balder version of Mr. Morton. Brian and Edie had the tables folded up, but they were still on the floor, along with the folding chairs, and the plants were still set up.

"What's going on here?" Harold asked. He looked around the room, a bit confused and a bit horrified. He really did seem to have a stick up his butt.

"Just business as usual, Harold," said Andy, wiping down the counter.

"I mean, what's with these tables and ferns?"

Brian stepped forward. "Cookies," he said.

Harold looked over at him. "Cookies?" he asked.

"Yeah," said Brian. "Girl Scout cookies. My little sister had about thirty boxes left over, and we set up a table here to sell them off. We just sold the last box a minute ago, so we're packing up."

"You guys look a little old to sell Girl Scout cookies," Harold said.

"A little male, too. I'm just saying," said Brian.

"All the actual Girl Scouts are out on a winter jamboree this weekend in Shaker Heights," I said.

Harold stared at me. "And the ferns?"

"We thought they were a nice touch."

Harold looked back up at Andy. "Did you allow them to set up like this?"

Andy shrugged. "I didn't see the harm," he said casually. "The Girl Scouts are a fine organization, and I know Wackfords wants to be involved with the community. They were going to set up in the parking lot, like usual, but I couldn't let them freeze to death."

"Well, you need to clear these things ahead of time!" said Harold, somewhat exasperated. "We can't set up anything here without clearing it with corporate first, and no third-party flyers or signs are allowed. That means no tables and cookie sales, either."

"There's no harm done, though," said Andy.

"We do things *by the book* here," said Harold. "And the book doesn't say anything about this."

"Are you the boss around here?" Coach Hunter asked. He was standing off to the side, still looking confused.

"Yes, I am, sir," said Harold, turning toward him. "How can I help you?"

"This place is out of control!" he muttered. "Whole town's out of control! I've got kids sneaking depressing poems into my office, and when I try to come here for a drink, I get people talking about something to do with accounting and management crap, this guy behind the counter gives me a cup of foam, and then some *skinhead punk rocker* comes and tells me to be hip!"

"Skinhead?" asked my dad. "I lost my hair in a chemistry accident. I'm not a racist or anything."

"Oh?" said Coach Hunter. "And I suppose you're going to tell me that your hair was dyed green as part of a science experiment?"

"All right, sir," said Harold. "I'm sure we can work this out."

"Maybe you should do some push-ups," Brian suggested from behind the camera. "That might make you feel better."

Coach Hunter moved his glare over to Brian—he looked like he was just longing to tell him to do some form of calisthenics, but since he was off school property, his powers were pretty useless. Truly, here stood a broken man. He was actually starting to look the way he was described in Dustin's poems: sad, confused, and scared, now that he was in a situation where push-ups were not the answer and any blows on his whistle would have been just unwanted, ineffective background noise. A vein in his neck was twitching, and I would have wailed with joy if I hadn't been starting to fear for my life. The guy looked like he was about three twitches from turning into the Incredible Hulk.

Then he looked over at Anna and me. Then he looked over at the guy doing regular office work, who was paying him no mind, and then over at the stapler. He stared good and hard at the stapler, and I thought for a second he was going to crack. I'm no psychologist, but in movies it's always a little thing, like running out of milk or finding out there's a hole in your socks, that pushes people over the brink. Maybe the sight of a familiar-looking stapler was the thing that was going to do it to Coach Hunter. Only a guy who was close to losing it would be as quick to shout at someone over climbing a rope or square-dancing as he was, after all.

Then Jenny broke the silence.

"Go to hell," she said timidly.

Coach Hunter looked away from the stapler and over at her, slowly leaning closer, like he was trying to get her in focus.

"What did you say?" he asked.

"I said go to hell," she said in a very small voice.

He looked at her, and then at my dad, and then at the stapler, and then back at her, like a guy in a movie on the Count Dave show beholding the creature as it first rises from the swamp. Jenny looked incredibly nervous.

"I'm really sorry, sir," said Harold. "Can I get you another drink?"

Coach Hunter looked up at Harold, then slowly shook his head.

"Out of control," he said.

And Coach Hunter sighed and walked out of the store.

"What the heck was his problem?" my dad asked. "That guy looked miserable."

"That was Coach Hunter. He's the gym teacher at school," I said.

"Oh," Dad said, as though it suddenly made pretty good sense. "Well, that stands to reason. I'd be miserable, too, if I were a gym teacher."

"You want to explain to me what that was all about, Andy?" asked Harold.

"No big deal, Harold," said Andy. "Just one of those guys who doesn't expect a cappuccino to be mostly foam. He was having a pretty bad day, I guess. Driving through the snow has everybody in a bad mood."

"That's what I figured," said Harold. He turned toward Anna and me. "But you guys need to clear out."

"Don't worry," I said. "We're all done, and we're just packing up. Right, guys?"

Everyone nodded. We stashed the tables and the water-cooler in the back room so Andy could get them home later. I stuffed the motivational posters in the trash. That just left the filing cabinet and the ferns to be taken away. We started to pile them together. The guy who was working on finance was still there, still not paying any attention. My dad watched the whole thing, looking a bit confused.

177

"I'll explain later," I muttered to him.

"Andy," said Harold, "we'll talk some more about this after your shift."

"No problem," said Andy. "Good luck, guys!" He waved at us.

We all shook hands with Troy and Andy, I waved goodbye to my dad, who looked a little puzzled but wasn't saying anything, and we were all out the door—including Jenny, who followed along just behind.

Jenny, in fact, practically skipped her way out of the store. "Did you hear that?" she asked. "I can't believe I said that! Wasn't it awesome?"

"That rocked," said Anna. "I've always wanted to tell that guy to go to hell."

"He never expected it coming from me!" said Jenny gleefully. She was actually jumping up and down now.

She'd just stood up to authority for the first time. I was getting used to doing it, but for her to do it . . . well, that really *was* pushing the bounds of reality.

In the parking lot, Mr. Streich was just getting out of his car.

"Hey, guys," he said, a bit surprised to see us. "Working on your movie?"

"Yep," I said. "We wanted to get some shots of the new downtown for contrast."

"Good idea." Streich nodded thoughtfully. "I'm just here to meet up with your dad."

"So I hear," I said. "He's already in there."

"Great," said Streich. "I wondered if he'd make it through the snow. Barely did myself! I'll see you guys on

178

Friday!" And he walked off. If Harold had stopped ranting and raving, Mr. Streich would probably end up none the wiser that ten minutes earlier, the Wackfords had been an accounting and midlevel management strategies office. Dad would surely tell him something weird was going on, but he'd take that in stride.

The snow was still coming down, though not nearly as hard as it had been earlier that morning, and there were plows rolling down Cedar Avenue.

"Well," I said to Anna, Brian, and Edie, "I guess that's a wrap."

"Well done," said Anna. "We managed to get plenty of footage, and we didn't even get arrested."

"Hang on," said Brian. "One more shot."

And he picked up his camera and aimed it at the front door of the Wackfords.

The pirate flag was still there, flapping in the snow.

Brian filmed it getting smaller and smaller as we walked away.

14

Well, that was it. Our career as pirates lasted about four hours, and at the end of it, I'd annoyed a gym teacher, seen my father accused of being a skinhead punk, struck a blow against what Edie always called "the corporate takeover of America," added experience in accounting and midlevel management strategies to my resume, filmed the better part of a movie, and acquired an official girlfriend—not bad, considering I'd done it all before the time I normally woke up on a Saturday.

We were all pretty excited on the walk away from the store, but no one was more excited than Jenny. She could hardly stop skipping and saying, "I can't believe I said that!"

We walked to my house first, since I lived the closest and we all needed to warm up. We dropped off the plants and filing cabinet, then headed straight down to Douglas and Venture to take some establishing shots of the old downtown—something to compare and contrast with all the shots we had of Cedar Avenue. It had stopped snowing by then, which would make the contrast even better. The air would be clear in the shots of the old downtown, where the fresh snow lent an additional bit of charm, while the retail wasteland shots would almost look like they'd been filmed in Siberia or something.

"Man," said Brian as we walked into Sip, "this is going to be a pain in the ass to edit. We've got, like, six hours worth of footage between the two cameras to wade through and put into a movie short enough to show in class."

"Who says it has to be that short?" I said. "We can make it a regular-length movie and just show a trailer for it as the presentation. Then they'll all have to see the whole thing separately. They're all going to want to."

We roamed through the shop to our usual table, and Trinity danced her way over to us.

"What happened?" she said. "You pirates didn't stab Troy and bury him at sea, did you?"

"Oh no," I said. "We're friendly pirates."

"I'm not!" said Edie.

"Okay, well, we aren't the violent kind."

"Unless provoked," said Edie.

"And there's no sea to bury him in anywhere near here," I said. "Unless you count the pond. And that's frozen."

"Whatever," said Trinity. "And he didn't get fired or arrested or anything, right?"

"Nope," said Brian proudly. "We told his boss we were selling Girl Scout cookies, and he fell for it."

Trinity chuckled. "You met Harold, huh?"

"Yeah," I said.

"And I told a teacher to go to hell!" said Jenny proudly.

"Wow," said Trinity. "Just don't start climbing on the tables again, okay?"

"Anyway," I asked, "do you mind if we record some things here in the store?"

"Be my guest."

We wandered around, filming the inside of Sip. We asked the few customers who had braved the snow why they came to Sip instead of the Wackfords, and they all had pretty much the same answer: they liked going someplace that was *their* place, not just another link in a large chain. One woman said she felt like she was just in a glorified Burger Box when she went to Wackfords. That was movie gold, right there.

"Well," said Edie to Trinity as we finished up, "I hope we can help you stay in business."

"What do you mean?" asked Trinity.

"Aren't you having trouble staying open with a Wackfords to compete with?"

"Are you nuts?" asked Trinity. "You talked to all those people at Wackfords, right?"

Edie nodded.

"Do you think any of them would have been caught dead here in the first place? And do you think any of our customers are going to go to the Wackfords?"

"Well . . . no," said Edie.

"See?" said Trinity. "We're doing fine."

"Oh," said Edie. Honestly, she looked kind of disappointed that Sip wasn't going out of business. I was a little surprised to hear this myself, but I guess it made pretty good sense.

"Wait a minute!" I said. "I heard George telling Troy you guys were closing in six months! That's part of why we did the takeover!"

"George is always saying that," said Trinity. "It's just to bother Troy. We aren't going anywhere."

"You said you had to sleep with him in the back room to get company secrets out of him!"

Trinity snickered. "I think that's excuse number two hundred and thirty-six."

I was relieved, of course, but more embarrassed than relieved. I'd just taken over a Wackfords, possibly risking jail time, to save a coffee shop that didn't even need saving. After a while, though, the embarrassment was gone, and I was just relieved that Sip wasn't closing.

"We aren't out of the woods yet," Anna said as we sat down. "Someone could still call and complain. We could still be in trouble."

"There weren't that many people," said Brian. "And only a couple of them didn't get a drink in the end."

"One is all it takes," I said. "We just risked some serious trouble to save Sip, and it didn't even need saving."

"That wasn't why we did it," said Anna. "It was never going to do that, anyway. We did it to make a point about the new downtown."

"And to bring down big business!" said Edie.

This brought Anna into a little argument with Edie over exactly what we'd hoped to accomplish with the whole thing, but the truth was that there were a lot of reasons. We'd done it out of frustration over poor city planning that had caused our part of town—Anna's and mine, anyway—

to go from being the main part of town to an afterthought. Out of despair from thinking our favorite place was closing. To make a good movie and a monument to the old downtown. And in my case, to prove to myself that I had the guts to do it.

Brian and Edie stuck around after that so Edie could beg Trinity for some tango lessons, and Jenny called to get another cab to take her home. She was still buzzed from having told Coach Hunter to go to hell.

Anna and I started walking home. We held hands the whole way, and when we got to her house, she grabbed me and kissed me long, and hard, and good.

"So," she said when we paused for a breath. "You never told me . . . Have you?"

"Have I what?"

"Seen a naked girl."

I pulled back a step and blushed about three different shades of red. "Well, define the conditions of seeing a naked girl," I said. "Do you mean, like . . . live and in person? Or just pictures?"

She laughed out loud. "I know you've seen pictures, dummy. Ever seen a real one, not counting, like, when you were a baby or anything? Your age or older."

"Well," I said, "I guess not."

I don't know exactly why this embarrassed me; I mean, it's not like there are a lot of nudie bars in the suburbs that let minors in, and I'm pretty sure air vents that offer a view of the girls' locker room only exist in a few of the best movies ever made.

"Didn't think so." She smiled.

"Same question to you," I said. "Have you seen a naked guy?"

"Sure," she said. "Sometimes when my dad is working at his office, I sit in on the life drawing group at the college. You know that. So I've seen naked guys and girls. Mostly college aged, some older."

"I can't believe they really let you into those."

"It's just an art class," she said. "No big deal. I've seen more erotic bug documentaries on public broadcasting."

"Yeah," I said, "but that means, you're like . . . one up on me."

"So?" She smiled.

"So . . . ," I said.

"So you're just going to have to live with it." She smirked. And she kissed me again, and walked into her house.

Anna was not one up on me, she was about a million up on me. Not only had she seen a lot more naked people than I had, or probably would in the near future, she also knew all about art and movies I'd barely even heard of. She played classical music with her parents while I was at home listening to my dad butcher "Smoke on the Water," which, honestly, should not be an easy thing to butcher. She was sophisticated and cool, and I was just a suburban slob being raised by a pair of dorks.

But she liked me. And she was kissing me.

If I didn't know better, I'd even say she liked to think of me as a bit of a dork. And not even in a condescending way.

That evening, Mr. Streich came over to my house with a bass guitar. This was the first time I could recall ever having a teacher in my house, and even though I liked the guy a lot

185

more than I had at the beginning of the year, it was still awkward, especially when I had to hear him and my dad trying to harmonize on "Day Tripper." The Wildewood Singers probably did it better. But Mr. Streich didn't ask me about the takeover, so I assumed that he hadn't found out, which was a relief.

To my even greater relief, he left before Dad put on his True American gear, though if he'd stayed, maybe he could have told Dad ahead of time that trying to grill indoors can cause a fire. He was a science teacher, after all. Not that you should need an advanced degree to know that starting fires indoors isn't the safest thing you could try. Luckily, Mom talked him out of the idea just before he lit the match.

It started snowing again that night, and it kept coming down on Sunday, enough that we actually got a snow day from school on Monday. The roads being too snowy for the buses didn't stop us from moving around ourselves; I went over to Brian's house, where we got a jump start on editing.

By midweek, we were deep into editing the footage of the takeover into a pretty good movie. Edie found out from Trinity, who found out from Troy, that a couple of people had called the store to complain that there'd been kids bugging them, but the complaints weren't really about us—they were about Andy, and most of the customers, like the lady in the tacky suit, weren't taken very seriously, even by Harold. After all, if they fired everyone people complained about, there'd be no employees left in town.

In fact, the only customer who really got Andy in

trouble was a woman, presumably Mrs. Smollet, who called the corporate office to say that he'd called her an idiot. Andy had happily offered his resignation before Harold could fire him.

On Friday, Coach Hunter apparently found some more poems in his office, because, true to his word, right after lunch, he enacted a locker search of everyone in the gifted pool. It was all done very quietly; he didn't gather the whole school together to watch or anything, like they do on TV. I only knew about it because as I was walking between classes, I saw the janitor opening James Cole's locker. Coach Hunter dug around for a bit, but the only thing he found was a large piece of paper taped to the inside of the door on which James had written "Hi, Coach!" He dug around, found nothing else besides a coat and gloves, and slammed the door shut. Locker slamming, of course, was strictly against the rules for students.

At the pool meeting that afternoon, Mr. Streich asked if we were all aware that our lockers had been raided that afternoon.

"Yes," I said. "Coach Hunter was behind it."

"That's right," said Mr. Streich. "And I imagine you all know what he was looking for. Dustin, James, I'm looking at you guys in particular."

"Did he find anything?" asked Dustin.

"No," said Mr. Streich. "And for the record, I have a bit of a problem with him deciding to search your lockers because he suspects somebody's writing poems. There's nothing illegal about writing poems, and singling you guys out just on a hunch is a little dicey. So I haven't told him what kind of project you guys said you were working on." I imagine that would give him quite a clue.

"Thanks!" said James.

"However," he continued, "I can imagine that you guys know pretty well who's responsible for the poems he's been finding in his office?"

"Do you know how many he's found?" asked Dustin.

"As of lunch today, he says he's found fourteen of them."

"Fourteen!" I said. "That's pretty impressive."

"Well," said Mr. Streich, "the problem is, you're sort of walking that fine line between pulling a prank and stalking. I'm going to go ahead and let you guys do your project about making a tombstone for him, and I'll refrain from ratting you out on two conditions."

"I'm willing to negotiate," said Dustin.

"Number one," said Mr. Streich, "you have to stop sending him the poems and trying to depress him. That goes without saying. Number two is that, in addition to making the tombstone, you and James will both be delivering eulogies for him at the presentation—nice ones. And you can't call him by name as part of the project, it has to be for an anonymous gym teacher. I could get in trouble myself over this."

That, I had to admit, was pretty clever. Tough, but fair.

"That's going to be hard," said Dustin. "Saying nice things about him?"

"We always say nice things about the dead," said Mr. Streich. "Even if you didn't like them. If I speak at my mother-in-law's funeral, I won't be saying a word about her having horns."

"Well," said James to Dustin, "I'm game if you are."

"Deal," Dustin sighed.

"In that case," said Mr. Streich, "congratulations on writing some fine poems. Hang on to them; I'm sure you'll find a way to use them for something eventually. You kept copies, right? Somewhere other than your locker?"

"Yeah," said Dustin. "And if he says that there's been fourteen of them so far, then he still has three more to find in his office."

We all laughed. "I'll let those slide," said Mr. Streich, nodding. "Anybody else making progress on their projects?"

"We are," said Brian. "I have a sample ready to show."

We had been working the whole week editing the takeover footage into something coherent, and we spent most of the rest of the class watching what he had. There were shots of Edie flicking off the the whole street in the snow—which turned out really well—shots of us walking up to the Wackfords and of the pirate flag flapping in the breeze. Then there were some scenes of annoyed customers, and scenes of us having business meetings and stuff, while that guy who was working on finances sat in the corner, not seeming to notice that anything weird was going on at all.

When the footage ended and Mr. Streich turned the lights back on, he looked pretty pale.

"So," he said, "you guys didn't tell me you were actually going to take over the Wackfords."

"The shift supervisor let us," said Brian. "We didn't threaten anybody or anything."

"And there were hardly any customers, anyway," I said. "And the supervisor was trying to get fired. He already took the rap."

"Did you get any of the customers to sign release forms?" asked Mr. Streich.

"Um, no," I said, kicking myself for having forgotten that.

"Then all that footage with the customers is useless," said Mr. Streich. "If you blur their faces out, you might get away with it, but even then, you could be in some serious trouble for this."

"But this isn't the whole movie," I said. "It's just a very rough draft of the part that takes place in the new downtown."

"And that footage of Edie in the street is fantastic!" said Anna.

"Well, yeah, that's pretty good," said Mr. Streich. "I tell you what. Finish the movie, but let me see it before you show it to anybody, anywhere. Got it?"

"Okay," I said. We still had plenty of work to do, anyway.

That night, we took the camera with us to Sip during the basketball game to film Dustin reading "Lonesome Whistle," the final poem in his "Theoretical Death of a Gym Coach cycle." He dressed in a black turtleneck for the occasion, and actually drank coffee instead of a smoothie, though he just nursed one cup the whole night, and I'm not sure he drank even half of it.

We shot a short interview with Trinity in which she

talked about the coffee industry's responsibility to local culture and talent, however questionable the talent may actually be, then filmed her introducing "the one, the only, the
irrepressible Dustin Eddlebeck, poet laureate of Cornersville
Trace Middle School."

Dustin bowed so deeply I thought he was going to fall
over, then began to read very dramatically, snapping his fingers the whole time.

"So long, Coach,
we'll all remember you, how you
yelled yourself blue
while we ran in vulgar circles,
every time we hear that lonesome whistle blow.
We'll think of the crack of the thick plastic mats
where the wrestling team got ringworm
every time we hear that lonesome whistle blow.
We'll think of the scream of the rubber
machines,
the smell of old socks
that followed us through the locker rooms,
and the fundamentals,
it all comes down to fundamentals,
every time we hear that lonesome whistle blow.
When we're walking along the
pockmarked sidewalks
down Seventy-sixth Street, on the way to Venture
and whatever's left of the old downtown,
skeleton frames, gravestones
underneath a blanket of brown leaves,

and we feel like we ought to hurry,
run faster, jump farther,
before the last of it is blown away,
we'll think of you, Coach. We'll think of you.
Every time we hear that lonesome whistle blow."

Brian and I then spent the weekend working our butts off editing the whole thing. In the end, the movie opened with a few scenes of Sip and the rest of the traingle that showed how cool the old downtown was, then contrasted that with shots of the retail wasteland on Cedar and some interviews and voice-overs about how the strip malls were taking over the town (like my slime that ate Cornersville Trace comment).

The takeover took up just a few minutes of the movie. We cut all the shots of customers getting harassed and edited it to look as though the place was practically deserted, which, given the weather, was no real trick, since the weather had kept most people away. The only customer we left in was the guy who'd stayed the whole time, looking oblivious while we acted like the place was an accounting office. Since he was there every day, Troy was able to get him to sign a release form.

To finalize the thing, Dustin and Anna recorded some piano and cello music to serve as background during the quieter scenes, and to serve as the music Edie was conducting with her middle fingers in the middle of Cedar Avenue as the morning snow fell. We ended up opening with that scene.

True to our word, we gave the first copy to Mr. Streich, who watched it during his planning period one day, then sent out messages through the office for Anna, Brian, Edie, and me to meet him in the pool room.

"You guys," he said as we walked in the door, "you've done a fine job on this. If I were a film critic, I'd say that I didn't really understand what the whole thing about having an accounting office in Wackfords is, exactly, but you at least show that that one guy can't seem to tell the difference, so it works."

"Then our work is done," said Anna.

"Well, one more thing," said Mr. Streich. "I have to ask you to promise not to put this thing out for distribution online or anything. If the Wackfords guys get ahold of this, you could still get in trouble. You probably already would be, if more people had come in. You dodged some major bullets."

"Why don't we have it be sold exclusively at Sip?" I said. "In a way, the whole thing is a commercial for Sip, and just a few sales there probably won't get back to Wackfords too soon."

"We'll see," he said. "We'll see."

Later that day, I gave James the stapler back, and he slipped it into Coach Hunter's office that evening, hiding it in the corner under some papers, so that when Coach Hunter ran across it, he might just think he'd misplaced it. Sure enough, when I came into gym the next day, Coach Hunter was in his office, happily stapling things. His mood was so good that he only made me do a couple of extra laps that day. By the end of the week, between having his stapler back and noticing that the poems weren't showing up quite so regularly, he was back to his old, slightly less-miserable self.

Two weeks later came the night when we all presented

our monuments. Dustin and James had erected a large tomb-stone (actually Styrofoam spray-painted to look like a rock) marked COACH. It was an obelisk nearly five feet high. Dustin read his "Lonesome Whistle" poem, and James gave a little speech about how he'd always remember "the un-known gym coach" fondly as a man who really took dodge-ball and square-dancing seriously—after all, when a person has a mission in life, it's hard not to respect them for it. Most of the people probably didn't know they were talking about a real gym coach who wasn't even dead.

After everyone else had shown their monuments, we showed the movie in its entirety—and got a standing ovation.

For a formerly avant-garde filmmaker like myself, it felt very strange to get that sort of mainstream acceptance.

Naturally, Coach Hunter found out about the tribute a couple of days later. He had Dustin and James both brought in to the principal, but since there was no rule against sneaking poems into someone's office, he had to content himself with being especially hard on them in gym class in-stead of having them thrown into reform school.

Right around the end of January, Mr. Streich decided it would be safe if we offered copies of the movie at Sip, so we printed up a few and talked George into selling them. We only sold a few in the first week, but it was a start.

In early February, word that I had a product on the market got back to Mr. Morton and the rest of his hangers-on at the Skills for the Job Market activity, and suddenly, I was the most popular kid in class. Most of the kids in the room thought that antagonizing big business like that was un-American (even though I knew that I was a True American, since I was a grilling one), but apparently, being able to market a movie, even just in a local business, meant that I had skills for the job market up the wazoo. In fact, I could probably use "wazoo stuffed with job market skills" as one of the bullet points on my resume.

Mr. Morton made me spend a whole class period telling the story of my success.

"Well," I said early on, "when you start a venture like this, they usually tell you to have a mission statement or something."

"Right!" said Mr. Morton proudly. "And what was yours?"

"Actually," I said, "it was 'Mission statements suck.'"

He seemed a bit put off by this, but I knew I was still getting an A.

To boost sales, we had a free screening of the movie at Sip. Troy and Trinity were both there, along with Andy, who was now working at a record store in one of the newer strip malls. Troy had managed to keep his job at Wackfords, where he planned to stay for exactly one more month before moving on.

Several people from the pool came, too, including Jenny, who had taken to following me around at a comfortable distance and staring at me from down the hall when she didn't think I was looking. Clearly, she wasn't over her crush. Just to be polite, Anna and I tried not to kiss in front of her. But since we'd both seen the movie several times already, we spent a good deal of the screening making out.

"This movie isn't really avant-garde at all, is it?" I asked Anna midway through.

"It's postmodern," said Anna.

"What's postmodern?" I asked.

She shrugged. "It's a theory that you can make up as you go along, really," she said. "But I know it when I see it, and this is it. We've moved on from our avant-garde phase." And she gave me a quick kiss and went back to watching the movie.

We'd moved on, all right.

For our first Valentine's Day as an official couple, Anna and I decided to spend the small amount of money we'd made off the sales of the movie on a trip to the city. Her dad drove us to a place called the Mercury Café, which was like a larger version of Sip that featured live jazz music. We sipped espresso and watched the band while her dad ate by himself at the bar to give us some privacy. Anna assured me that the band was pretty bad, as jazz bands went—in fact, her exact words were that they "sucked cheese"—but I'd never felt so sophisticated in my entire life.

"This is the life," I said. "Hanging out in the city, listening to music, and sipping coffee. That's what it's all about."

"Yeah," she said. "Nothing against Sip or anything, but I prefer the city to any part of Cornersville Trace."

"I know what you mean," I said. "And we're stuck there until college, at least."

"Just a few more years to go," she said.

"A few long, long years," I said.

She kissed me on the cheek. "We'll make the best of it, I guess," she said.

It was after midnight when her dad drove us back home, so most of the lights on Cedar had been turned off, and if it hadn't been for the blue glow from the Mega Mart sign shining on them, I could almost have imagined that the streetlights were the vanished trees that had been there before, back when the early explorers and trappers came through and found nothing but dark, imposing wilderness where the Burger Box now stood.

The only trees now were the small ones that had been planted on the edges of the parking lots, where the cars of a few late-night employees were still sitting. I didn't need a crystal ball to guess that my friends and I would probably all be McHobos ourselves by the end of high school, working one crappy job after another in the strip malls of Cedar Avenue, trying to make the best of it.

But if the movie had proved one point, it was that we could stand up to those places.

I was so lost in thought, thinking of all that and staring at Anna, with all of the blue and green and red signs reflecting in her glasses again, that if we hadn't pulled to a stop at the traffic light near the Wackfords, I wouldn't have noticed that Troy was in there, closing the place down for the night.

When I looked closer, I saw that Trinity was in a car in the parking lot, waiting for him. And I saw that he'd put Edie's skull and crossbones flag up on the flagpole, where it was waving in the winter wind.

About the Author

Born in Des Moines and now based in Chicago, Adam Selzer worked twenty or thirty retail and restaurant jobs between eighth grade and the year after college. His first book was *How to Get Suspended and Influence People*, also published by Delacorte Press. Today he works as a "weird tour guide," assistant ghost buster, and part-time rock star. Check him out on the Web at www.adamselzer.com.